A Lullaby for Toby

BY TOM REYNOLDS

ISBN: 978-0-578-50131-4

CREDITS:
[1]Gould, Stephen Jay, *Dinosaur in a Haystack*, p.222.
[2]Gordon Bok, "Isle au Haut Lullaby," (Sharon, Connecticut: Folk Legacy Records, 1999), © 1965 Gordon Bok, BMI used by permission.
[3]Rilka, Rainer Maria. *Letters to a Young Poet*, Translated by Charlie Louth, (New York: Penguin Books 2013), p. 24.

Acknowledgments

A special thanks to Susan St. John, who edited the first draft, and Melanie M. Austin, who did the final copy edit of this book.

I also want to thank my wife, Claudia McNeill, for reading and commenting on the first draft, and for her patience with what turned out to be almost a three-year process of writing, revising, and marketing the book. Finally, I want to thank Ellen Martorelli, Suellen Mele, Jim Nelson, and Monica Wood for their interest and encouragement throughout the writing process.

Contents

Part 1

Maine, August 2008

Chapter One

Something Lost

I'm dreaming about Keira and Kelly, the two girls I hang out with at West Lake High. Now I know what you're thinking—this guy must be a real Romeo. But it's not like that. I'm not ready yet to have just one special girlfriend, someone to spend all my time with, someone I'm *serious* about. And both these girls, each in her own way, are a lot of fun. Besides, all three of us sing in the West High choir. And when you sing together, you hang together. So it's only normal we would be friends.

"Wake up Robbie!" A shadow passes over me, and I half open my eyes.

Someone is standing by the bed. I can't quite make out who. Bright sunlight is streaming in through the big window next to the bed, and for a moment it blinds me. Then I see it's Toby, my little sister. She's giving me the look I know all too well—she wants me to do something.

"Get up," she says, in her best whiny voice. "I want to go exploring on the little island."

Mom, Dad, Toby, and I are in Maine, spending our summer vacation at my grandfather's. We usually go to Orcas Island, about a two-hour car and ferry ride from our house in Seattle, Washington. Mom's boss lets her use his summerhouse a couple of weeks each summer. That makes it easy for Mom, a home mortgage officer for a company called America's Dream, to be in constant contact with her office. Since spring she has also spent a lot of time volunteering for the Obama campaign.

So finally, I guess, Dad just got fed up and decided to break the pattern. "We need a real vacation," I heard him telling Mom. And that is how we ended up all the way across the country this year—that, and because Mom was feeling guilty about not visiting Granddad Bill in eight years.

Bill has a big white house in Clyde Hill overlooking Penobscot Bay. He calls it a New Englander. If you check Google Images, you'll find pictures of other "New Englanders," all of which seem to be in Maine." It sits on a small hill—the original Clyde Hill according to Bill—and has a wide set of steps leading up to a big front porch that looks out toward the bay. On the first floor, there is a living room, a dining room, a kitchen, and a bedroom. The house has a large pointed roof, and the first time you see it from the front, you think the second floor must be pretty big. But when you climb up the narrow stairs from the first floor, you're surprised by how little it is: just two small bedrooms and a tiny half bathroom, along with a little alcove at the end of a narrow hall just past the bedrooms. You see, all the space is in the attic. Bill's house has a huge attic.

It's hard to think of Bill as my grandfather. He's a retired Unitarian minister. That's all I really know about him. We haven't been here for a visit since I was nine. The last time was for my grandmother Helen's funeral. Mom wanted us to come out to help her "take care" of her Dad. That was before she became so busy with her work. Anyway, all Granddad Bill kept saying was that she didn't understand, and that she hadn't been around enough to know what was going on. I don't think he really wanted to be taken care of, and after a week or so, Mom seemed to get the message, and we went back home. Since then, the only times we've talked have been over the telephone when Bill calls Mom or vice versa. But we never had much to say during those short conversations.

I'd just turned seventeen when Dad got this idea that we should visit Maine again for a "real" vacation. He called Granddad Bill, who agreed to let us stay for two weeks in August.

Right off shore, about a quarter mile from Bill's house, is this tiny island. It's not much of an island, just one long pile of rocks, really, with some soil and a couple of scrub trees at its widest point. But Toby has been pestering us since we got to Bill's to go out to the island. And by *us* I really mean *me* because I'm the one who is supposed to watch out for Toby when Dad and Mom are busy.

Today is Friday, the end of our first week. I was up late stargazing with Dad and Granddad Bill. Bill has a friend with a home telescope that looks east. Dad teaches astronomy, and we both love looking at the night sky, particularly when we get a chance to stargaze away from the bright lights of the big city.

I was hoping to sleep late, but I know now that's not going to happen. I glance at my watch, sitting on a stack of books next to the bed. It's 10:00 a.m.—late but I still feel tired. I look back at Toby, and I can tell from the look on her face that I'm not going to get any more sleep. My little sister can be such a pain. Sometimes I wish she would just disappear.

Did I promise to take her over to the island this morning? I can't remember, but it doesn't matter because we are going anyway. So I push my feet over the edge of the bed and get up.

I sleep in one of the small bedrooms upstairs. The room felt really cramped the first couple nights I was here. But now I've kinda gotten used to it. The big window by the side of the bed had a nice view of the small forest of trees on the south side of the house and of the shabby little garden in the back yard. I guess it used to be Helen's garden. But now it's just kind of a mess, although I can tell someone has been weeding on the west side.

The upstairs ceiling is cut at a sloping angle, and whenever I walk over to look out the window, I risk banging my head. All the Saunders are tall: Bill, Mom, and me included. Height is the one thing I inherited from my mother. Everything else came from Dad.

"Did you have breakfast?" I ask as I stumble past Toby and into the tiny bathroom with its little sink and a toilet.

She shakes her head, turns and heads for the stairs. A bird is singing full throttle outside. It sounds like a robin, and for a minute I think I'm back home. I pull on my jeans and the same plaid shirt I wore on Thursday, grab my MP3 player and head downstairs. The first thing I see is Toby sitting at the kitchen table with a glass of milk like she is waiting to be served. Sitting by her on the table is her little pink sun hat and her little pink camera.

As I sit down, I immediately notice someone has left a folded piece of paper in the middle of the kitchen table with my name written on it. A note from Dad, I guess.

"Dad and Grandpa Bill went into town," Toby says. The town in this case is Belfast. I leave the note sitting on the table—I'll read it in a minute. Right now, I'm thinking about food.

Someone, probably Dad, has made oatmeal with blueberries. But the oatmeal is now sitting cold in two bowls by the microwave. I haven't seen Mom. She's probably in Bill's workroom, using her laptop or maybe talking on her iPhone. I get some OJ out of the fridge, heat one bowl of oatmeal in the microwave, and give it to Toby. Then I heat mine. For a moment, we both stare at our food, and Toby sort of plays with hers using her spoon. Finally, we both dig in. It doesn't take long for us to wolf everything down. I put the bowls in the sink. Then I grab a couple of apples and two cartons of yogurt from the fridge, along with two beach towels, and we head out the door.

Toby hasn't stopped talking about the little island since she first saw it. Mom and Bill had told her not to go near it without one of us along, and there hasn't been time the first week for what seems to me a very boring activity.

"You don't need to go out to that island," Mom had told Toby right after we got here. But Toby is her favorite, protected and fussed over as much as Mom could fuss over anybody. Anyway, Toby kept on talking about the island.

"I think there's a treasure out there," she would say, "or something mysterious. Please, oh please, can Robbie take me out to the island?"

I guess she's bored. She wants a little adventure, and everyone telling her no just makes her more determined than ever to go. Toby is like that. If she wants to do something, no one can stop her from making a pest of herself until she gets her way. And, as Mom always says, "She is too young to judge the risks." Or more likely, she just doesn't care. But isn't it about time Toby started listening to other people?

"It can be dangerous out there," Bill told us. "The island can shrink by a third when the tide comes in, and sometimes sneaker waves, or dumping waves, can form on the far side of the island because of the currents. These are dangerous. They can run over the edge of the island and sometimes pull swimmers under. If the weather changes too quickly, and you can't get back in, you could be in trouble."

But Toby just kept on talking about the island, So Dad finally suggested I take Toby out some morning when the tide was out. At first, I was glad that a decision had been made, but then she started pestering me every day about going.

"When can we go? When can we go?" She wouldn't shut up, so I guess maybe I finally blurted out that we could go in the morning if it was sunny, and we could get going early while the tide was still out. So now I'm stuck. OK, anything to stop her whining.

Before I stand up to go, I open the folded piece of paper that Dad, or somebody, has left on the kitchen table. There's nothing written inside. Odd, I think.

As we step out onto the porch, the sun seems unusually bright, and the bay looks like something off a picture postcard. Toby pulls on her floppy little sun hat and runs ahead of me toward Bill's canoe, sitting on the edge of the bay. It's already a hot day, and despite being tired, I'm glad to be outside. So here I am, taking my annoying little sister out to a little nothing of an island on a Friday morning when I should be sleeping late. For a minute, I think about knocking on the door to Bill's workroom to check with Mom before we go. But Toby is already well ahead of me, and Mom doesn't like to be disturbed if she's talking to Dan, her boss. So I just sprint ahead to catch up with Toby.

I'm already formulating a plan for the afternoon. On my player, I have a play list that includes a couple of songs our choir director, Mrs. Walker, has hinted we'll be singing in the fall. I need to start learning these songs because this year, I finally want to try out to sing a solo, and I need to be able to impress Mrs. Walker.

For an eight-year-old, Toby is all long arms and legs. You can already tell she's going to be tall, just like Mom. Hanging by an elastic strap from one arm, she has her small pink camera, a birthday present from my parents. It matches the little pink backpack and the sandals she's wearing. There is a funny little decorated cat face on both the backpack and the camera. It's something Mom helped Toby make and then attach to her stuff.

Toby is obsessed with taking pictures. Everywhere she goes, she drags that little camera along. At first, everybody thought it was so cute: Toby running around sticking her camera in everyone's face, stopping to shoot pictures of old houses, or a pretty flower, or an old fire hydrant. But when she started taking pictures of everything, and I mean everything—dead animals, the linoleum tile in our kitchen, Mom in her underwear—her picture-taking got old real quick. So after a while, Toby's camera use was limited, which became a cause for even more whining. I was hoping that Mom and Dad might make her leave the camera at home, but no such luck.

"Wait, Toby," I say, and increase my pace so I can get down to the shore before she tries to push the canoe into the water.

Bill calls the boat a canoe, but it's more like a small metal boat. I grab Toby and lift her into the canoe after one of her flip-flops gets caught on the rim, and she almost falls headfirst into the boat.

"I can do it," she says, as she squirms out of my hands, but only after I sit her down safely on the front seat of the canoe.

I toss in our towels and the small bag of food. Before I step into the canoe myself, I look out at the bay. The tide is going out—I'm sure of it. Should I go back and check the tide tables? Again, I remember the note on the kitchen table. It was probably from Dad. Had he left a tide table on the kitchen table by his note? No he hadn't. Maybe he expected me to use Granddad Bill's ancient Mac to check today's tides. That thing is so slow I can't stand it. Mom brought her laptop, but that's for her to use, and when she is using it, you don't dare interrupt her.

"Let's go!" Toby yells. "Let's go!"

"Ok, but first put this on." I hand her one of the life jackets Bill has stored in the boat.

She frowns and looks at me incredulously.

"Go ahead and put it on," I say. "We're not going anywhere until you do."

Finally, she puts on the life jacket.

I step into the canoe, sit down and then look out at the water again. The bay looks flat. I'm sure the tide is still going out.

"Aren't you going to put your life jacket on too?" she asks sarcastically. I can see that she's going to pester me about it until we get to the island. So I stop and slip mine on.

Rowing out to the island takes less than ten minutes. I think it's about eleven o'clock but I'm not really keeping track of the time. The day is getting hotter, and I'm starting to look forward to relaxing on the island and listening to my music.

There's no real grass on the island. The beach is covered with small rocks and pebbles, and the upper part of the island is packed dirt. But there is a long, thin patch of sand that runs from under the largest of the shriveled trees down the side of the island facing Bill's house, almost to the water. I pull the canoe over the pebbles and onto this small patch of sand. We spread our towels up by the stunted little tree at the center of the island. From here I can see both sides of the island.

I take off my backpack and life vest, and Toby does the same, dumping them by her towel.

"Do you want part of an apple?" I ask.

"No," says Toby, "I want to take pictures."

"Be sure you stay away from the water," I say. I look at Toby. She's not even listening to me.

"I'm serious."

She's staring out at the water. Then she spins around and starts taking pictures of the little tree. In the distance to the north, I notice some white puffy clouds. But above me the sky is a pristine blue. I watch Toby as she crawls around the top of the island. Move over Dorothea Lange, here comes Toby Steele. She looks completely ridiculous.

After standing and watching Toby for a few minutes, I start to feel tired. So I move my blanket to see her better as she moves to the landward side of the island and then sit down. I take a drink out of my water bottle and put on my headphones. Then I turn on my player.

"Look, Robbie!"

I glance over at Toby. She's holding her camera in one hand and staring out at the water. I turn around and look out over the bay. I notice a big boat, probably a yacht of some kind, sailing by. There's a strong wake right behind the boat.

"Get away from the water," I say, not very loud. Maybe I should get up. But it's so hot I just want to sit still. My head fills up with music. *Whoosh*. I notice a slight breeze. It feels nice. I start thinking about Keira and Kelly and how great my senior year is going to be. Suddenly, I'm really tired. I lie down on my towel but keep my eyes open.

Somewhere in the distance, Toby says, "Look, Robbie!"

I close my eyes and see Keira, her long dark brown hair sparkling in the light. Beautiful, talented Keira is model thin. Then red-headed Kelly appears, laughing as usual. Kelly's crazy funny. Mike Sakoda describes her as a "full-figured girl." He can be crazy funny too. As I'm thinking about Mike, he appears, joking about something or another.

In the corner of my eye, I notice a figure walking along the shore toward the bay side of the island. I start to say something but fall back into daydreaming about Keira and Kelly. Choir's going to be great this year, and so is school. I may even ace second-year Spanish. It feels like I'm smiling, but somewhere in my head, I know I can't be because I'm asleep.

Whoosh.

My MP3 player stops, and my eyes pop open. I'm thinking, *I shouldn't be nodding off.* I sit up and pull out my ear buds. Toby's towel is stretched out, slightly down the little hill from mine. Her pink backpack and life vest are still by her towel, but she's not there. My heart jumps. Water is lapping at the bottom edge of her towel. The tide is coming in. I jump to my feet.

"Toby!" I yell. There's no response. I don't see her anywhere on this side of the island. Immediately, I notice our canoe bobbing up and down about two feet offshore. She's got to be in the boat. I run down and splash into the water. It's not even a foot deep. But when I get to the boat it's empty. I step away from the canoe and look up and down the landward side of the island, but there's no Toby. I drag the boat back to the shore, yelling for Toby as I do.

I walk back up to the tree where we left our towels and look down the east side of the island. "Toby, if you're hiding somewhere, come out, or I'm going to kill you!" Then I turn and run around the south end of the island and back to the towels. There's still no Toby. Now my heart is racing. She's got to be here some-place, but where?

I take a couple of deep breaths, and stare out at the bay. There's no sign of Toby. The water is still rising, and I pick up Toby's towel and backpack and toss them closer to mine. I look at my watch. It's one o'clock. I've been asleep for almost two hours. How could that be?

"Toby! Toby!" There's still no answer. I run around to the south end of the island. My heart is racing again. She's not here. If she's hiding or playing some kind of a joke on me, I'll kill her. But where could she be hid-ing? She's not in the boat. There's no place to hide on the island.

I start shaking and fall to my knees. I feel sick. I'm scared, really scared. "Toby!" I scream. But there's no answer. She's not here. She's gone.

CHAPTER TWO

A Family Affair

I dash around the island one more time, but no Toby. Where is she? Frustrated and scared, I know I have to get help.

Bill and Dad are standing on the porch when I come racing up from the beach, after I've rowed back from the island. Breathless, confused, and speechless, I don't know what to say when Dad asks me, "Where's Toby?" I put my hands on my knees and try to catch my breath, needing to think, trying to figure out what happened.

"I don't know," I blurt out after a moment.

Dad looks a little confused. "You don't know?"

"I sat down to listen to my playlist. She was running around with that camera of hers, taking pictures, and the next thing I knew she was gone."

Both men look at me in disbelief.

"I closed my eyes for just a minute and when I opened them, she was gone."

"You closed your eyes?" Bill says slowly, as if he is trying to figure out what I'm talking about. Then he frowns. There's a moment of silence, and then Dad says, "Bill, Robin and I will go back to the island. Can you call the sheriff?"

"Sure. What about telling Claire?"

Dad shakes his head. "Wait until we get back."

On the way out to the island, I tell Dad my story: how Toby was wandering around taking pictures like she always does, how I watched her for a while then sat down to listen to my playlist, and how when I looked for her again, she was gone. As I try to explain what happened, I realize I'm in trouble. Dad is usually much cooler than Mom about most things, but I can tell from the look on his face that if we don't find Toby, and find her pretty quick, I'm going to face one big interrogation, or something even worse.

"I remember her saying something about wanting me to look at something, and I told her not to go down by the water. I told her twice."

Dad still doesn't say anything. He frowns and turns away to look at the island.

Once we get to the island, I show him where we were sitting. I can't help but notice how far the tide has come in. Dad catches me looking at the water. He knows what I'm thinking.

"You checked the tide tables before you came out, didn't you?"

I don't know what to say. Was there a tide table on the kitchen table with his note? I probably should have looked up the tides on Bill's old computer.

"I left a tide table pamphlet on the small table by the front door, Robin."

I never thought to look on that little table. Why didn't he leave it on the kitchen table, where he knew I would see it? I know an explanation won't help now, so I just mumble *shit* under my breath.

We walk around the island, but the result is the same—no Toby. The rising tide has washed away any footprints close to the water. Then we notice a line of prints leading from the biggest tree down toward the waterline on the east side of the island. They're from Toby's sneakers.

Dad takes out the small leather notebook he carries with him everywhere. He uses it to record things like the day's weather, facts about local geology, and astronomical observations, like the phases of the moon and what planets you can see on certain nights, with the naked eye or a pair of high-power binoculars. He writes something in the notebook.

Dad used to be an assistant professor in the Astronomy Department at the University of Washington. On the third floor of the Astronomy/Physics Building, where Dad had his office, there is a big picture of the Andromeda Galaxy, the biggest galaxy in the local group of galaxies that includes our Milky Way. Andromeda is a spiral galaxy about 250,000 light years across, which contains a trillion stars. The first time I saw it I was eight, the same age as Toby is now, and I was visiting Dad at his office. I remember thinking how beautiful it was and how small it made me feel.

Dad told me that in about four billion years the two galaxies would collide. What did it mean, I wondered? That was the first time I thought about how things end. Animals, people, planets, stars, even galaxies—everything ends. But it's different when someone you know gets lost or dies. It's personal then and it's really scary.

Dad looks up from his notebook and then stares out at the bay. The water now seems almost still, a sure sign the tide is starting to go back out. A few wispy clouds float by above us. Again, the bay seems completely at peace.

But when we get back to shore, a storm is waiting—Mom. She strides down toward us as we pull the canoe onto the land. Dad intercepts her. They exchange words. Then she breaks off and heads straight for me. Now the shit's going to fly.

"Robin, where's Toby?" The muscles in her face are tight, and she is clenching her teeth. I try to explain what happened, but she steps forward and raises her voice.

"I don't want to hear excuses. It was your responsibility to watch Toby. So what happened?"

"I don't know. I sat down to listen . . ." The look on her face stops me mid-sentence. For a minute, I think she is going to grab me.

"No excuses," she says. "Get back up to the house. Go to your room and stay there." Boy, I'm in so much trouble.

I walk past her and then Dad. Bill is standing on the front porch.

"No luck?" he asks.

"No," I say as I walk past him.

"Don't worry, Robin. I'm sure we'll find her."

Up in my room, I look out the big window at the trees. In this view of the world, everything is still peaceful. I hope Bill's right, but whether he is or not, I'm scared and confused. What's the worst thing that could happen? That my parents will never forgive me? That something terrible has happened to Toby? That she's dead? Or that it's my fault?

Now my stomach is aching. I sit down on the bed. *How could Toby be so stupid*? I want to scream. She always does what she wants to do. She is so selfish. Why couldn't she just listen to me and stay away from the water? That thought makes me turn cold. I know what everybody is thinking, Mom and Dad and now me. Everybody is thinking that Toby has drowned.

Downstairs, I hear people talking. Someone from the sheriff's office must have arrived.

I have to stop thinking about this. I grab my MP3 player, put in my ear buds, lie down, and start singing along with the first song. After a minute, my fears begin to fade. I love to sing; singing always makes me happy. We'll find Toby. I know it. And when we do, everyone will see that it wasn't my fault. Everyone will understand, and my last year at West Lake High will be just the way I've dreamed it would be. Maybe I'll even meet a new girl. Somebody more exciting than the girls I know at school. Somebody . . . But this is no time to be daydreaming about girls.

CHAPTER THREE

The Unexpected Child

Toby can be such a pain. This disappearance is classic Toby. I think it's mostly Mom and Dad's fault. From the day she was born, she's been at the center of my parents' world. Toby knows that and she milks it to get whatever she wants. Aunt Donna, Mom's older sister, calls her an unexpected child. But I remember how happy my parents were when she showed up, especially Mom. And right from the beginning, the unexpected child got special attention.

Then Dad left his job at the university—something that in my family is never talked about openly. It's just referred to as *The End*. I don't really understand why he left. I heard Mom and Dad talking about it a couple times, but when they realized I was listening, they either changed the subject or sent me outside. I heard enough though to know that he didn't exactly get fired. He didn't get something called tenure, and that had to do with some research he was doing on a mysterious planet. Writing about a mysterious planet sounded cool to me. But anyway, *The End* changed our lives in a big way.

Dad finally got a job teaching two classes, astronomy and geology, at Northshore Community College, but in the meantime, Mom returned to work. She had talked about going back to work before, but I'm not sure she was serious about it. For one thing, she loved taking care of her Toby. And for another, she was determined to see that the housework was done right. Anyway, when she went back to work full-time, Dad took over doing stuff around the house. But then he started picking up more classes and things at home got kinda crazy. Toby was almost five, and already she was becoming what Aunt Donna called "a handful." So after a while, Donna started to come over twice a week just to help out.

I was in my second year of middle school and was struggling grade-wise and every-other-wise. Before, Dad had always had time to help me with my schoolwork. But apparently, doing yard work, buying groceries, and teaching takes a lot of time because we got together less and less to talk about school stuff. I didn't push it because, frankly, some of the biggest challenges I had in middle school weren't with my classes. They were with girls and with the idea of being cool.

Meeker Middle School was a different world from elementary school. By eighth grade my middle school world was increasingly dominated by groups of other guys who were trying to be cool, and groups of girls whose goal was to look like they'd stepped out of *Teen* magazine. As Mike explained to me, there was a hierarchy that determined your status by eighth grade, and if you didn't rate on either one—or both—of the cool or hot lists, well, "Good luck, loser."

Life in middle school was confusing, and I really began to get irritated by the amount of attention Princess Toby was getting at home. Then she had to be rushed to the hospital to have her appendix out. Whoever heard of a five-year-old having her appendix taken out? But leave it to Toby to grab everyone's attention any way she can. Mom and Dad spent three days at the hospital, and then Mom tried working from home two days a week. Some days, with Mom, Aunt Donna, Dad, and a supposedly recuperating Toby at home, I felt like I was going crazy. I had trouble studying. But nobody seemed to notice because, more or less, I was just getting ignored.

After her operation, Toby became even more exasperating. She would interrupt people all the time, like the few times Dad and I got together to talk about school stuff. She would just walk into my room and start asking Dad questions, or want him to read with her.

Taking pictures is only one of Toby's obsessions. When she was six, she started bringing things home. First, it was animals: a dog, and then, over time, three cats. We kept them a while, and eventually found homes for the dog and one of the cats. Another one of the cats just disappeared. I always thought it probably found another home where the food was better, and it didn't have to put up with some little girl carting it around all day, but Toby concocted a story about the cat being eaten by wolves. Of course, there are no wolves in the city. There are coyotes but not wolves. Leave it to Toby to create a drama out of every little thing that happened in her life.

After the second cat disappeared, Toby made such a fuss that Mom and Dad decided it would be better to let her keep the third one. Maybe they thought taking care of the cat would teach her a lesson. Anyway, Moon Pie— so named because of the big white spot on her nose— joined our crazy household. Of course, over time, Toby moved on to other things, and Dad and I ended up taking care of Moon Pie, a quiet but friendly cat. She often comes to my room to sit on my desk and stare out the window. I've decided that she is probably smarter than her titular owner, Toby, because she knows a good thing when she's got it and acts accordingly.

But not even Toby's habit of bringing home stray animals could prepare my parents for the day Toby brought home a homeless girl named Lila. When she walked through the front door with Lila, I waited for Mom to explode, but because Toby was her special little girl, she didn't. My parents had a lot of questions, but Lila didn't seem able to tell us anything. She just smiled and shrugged when they asked her who her parents were or what her phone number and address were.

"Well, we've got to call the police," Dad said when it became clear that Lila wasn't going to tell them where she lived or why she had been sleeping in the park.

Toby immediately threw a hissy fit. "Can't she just stay downstairs," she whined.

"Honey," said Mom, "we don't know anything about her, and she doesn't seem to want to tell us where she lives or how we can contact parents."

A policewoman came to our house. She sat in our living room and asked Lila and my parents a lot more questions. Toby insisted on sitting in on the questioning. That was sure a mistake. She kept interrupting the policewoman until she was asked to either be quiet or leave the room. After that Toby sat with her arms folded and a big dark frown on her face.

When Lila left with the policewoman, Toby stormed off to her room. Later, when I went upstairs, I heard her crying. I can't ever remember Toby crying except for that one time, and I remember wondering why she was so upset.

CHAPTER FOUR

Girl with the Jet-Black Hair

I'm wandering along the shoreline, just trying to get away from the house and all the interrogation. The two Waldo County sheriff's deputies who came to the house asked us a bunch of questions. Could Toby swim? Yes. Were there life jackets in the boat? Yes. Why hadn't I made Toby keep hers on after we got to the island. Because she wasn't supposed to go into the water! Was Toby the kind of kid who would just go off on her own? Maybe. Had she ever run away from home? No.

I finally had to admit that I might have fallen asleep for a few minutes while I was supposed to be watching Toby—a few minutes, not almost two hours.

As the questions went on and on, I could see Mom getting more and more frustrated.

"Just go out and find her," she said finally.

As it turned out, Dad had to fill out an official report for the state police, and because I was the last one to see Toby alive, I had to sit with Dad and help him answer some of the questions. But going over and over the same things just made me feel more upset. I kept asking myself why hadn't Toby listened to me? How could she have gotten off the island? Why had I let myself go to sleep?

While one female deputy stayed with us, the other deputy left to walk along the beach and look for signs of Toby. I guess they're thinking she's in the water. But if that's the case, why aren't they looking there? Mom must be thinking the same thing because she's looking more and more upset—if that is possible.

"Can't you just get a boat and go look for her?"

"We're waiting for the state police boat to arrive, Mrs. Steele," said the female deputy. "It usually takes about twenty minutes."

Then she explained that the official missing persons report was the way the sheriff notified other police agencies across the state about Toby's disappearance. Once it was sent out, every police force in Maine would be looking for Toby.

Of course, this seemed overly bureaucratic because we were all thinking that Toby was in the water, and that was where they should be looking. Mom started to argue with the deputy. Then Dad stepped in and thanked the deputy for coming out so quickly and starting the search. I could tell Mom wasn't happy with that, but she must have decided that arguing wasn't speeding up the search because she stopped.

After they talked with my parents, the two deputies did start searching the shoreline in front of Bill's house for any sign of Toby. Then, at two o'clock, the sheriff's boat arrived, and they started the official search for Toby on and around the island. By then I was upstairs, hiding in my bedroom and trying to settle down.

But I was too nervous and just couldn't relax. I kept wondering how Toby had gotten off the island without my seeing her leave. When I couldn't just sit around any longer, I snuck out of the house. As I left, I heard Dad and Mom talking in the upstairs bedroom. Mom was really unhappy with me and with the police. Bill saw me leave. We made eye contact, but he didn't say anything.

It's after five now. The police boat has been slowly circling the island for a couple hours. The island looks calm—no different than it had this morning, except for the yellow incident tape strung around it. You wouldn't know that an eight-year-old girl had disappeared from there just a few hours ago. I notice a big bird circling the island. I vaguely remember seeing it when I was running around the island looking for Toby.

I just keep asking myself, why didn't Toby listen to me about going too close to the water? If she was caught in the current, why didn't I heard her call out for help? Could I have really fallen asleep for almost an hour? If this was some kind of Toby stunt to get everybody's attention, I'll never forgive her.

Warm late afternoon sunlight falls across the bay. I pace along, lost in my thoughts, until I notice someone is watching me. She is sitting at the top of a set of steps that come down to the shoreline from a large, rundown-looking house.

We make eye contact, but she's just a little too far away for me to see her clearly. I slow down and start to wander in her direction. She is wearing black jeans, the kind that have that intentionally tattered look, a simple knit top, and brownish trainers. She's slender, and she's got what looks like a sketchbook in her lap. Then, as I get closer, I notice her jet-black hair. The awfulness of today fades a little. *Who is this girl?*

"Hello," I say, trying to seem cheerful and nonchalant.

She gives me a blank look. Like maybe she's thinking about something else or is slightly sad. I can't tell.

Finally, she smiles, a soft smile that lights up her whole face. Then I notice her violet eyes and her breasts, which are slightly visible because the top button on her top is unbuttoned. Wow, this girl is spectacular.

"What's going on up the beach?" she asks as I get closer.

My brain is mush, a mixture of emotions and hormones. I can feel my heart beating. This is crazy.

"You know, with all the cops and the police boat around the island."

Suddenly, I'm back to thinking of Toby. "Someone is missing."

"Who?"

"My sister."

"Oh." She looks bewildered.

A moment passes, each of us apparently not knowing what to say. I feel conflicted. I'm totally captivated by this beautiful girl. But my brain is whispering, *What are you doing! Toby is missing, and you're trying to hook up with some girl you don't even know.*

"She was out on the little island and then she disappeared."

"How old is she?"

"Eight."

"Oh, so what was she doing out on the island?"

I can tell where this is going, and I don't want to go there, so I say, "Toby loves islands. We usually go up to an island in Puget Sound for our vacation—if we take one. And Toby goes crazy waiting for the trip."

"I can understand that feeling. One summer my parents took me out to Isle au Haut. We stayed at the inn and hiked all over the island. I fell in love with the place." Then she kind of shrugged and added, "Dad always promised to take me back. But that never happened."

I don't want to spoil the moment and lose my chance of finding out who this girl is. But I don't want to talk more about Toby, so I change the subject. "Anyway, my name is Robin—Robin Steele."

She gives me a questioning look. "Isn't that kind of upsetting? Your sister going missing and all."

"Yeah, that's why I had to get out and take a walk."

She thinks about my answer. Then after a minute she sticks out her hand. "I'm Maude."

Her hand is warm, really warm, and the warmth shoots through my body.

"Robin, that's an interesting name. Your parents must like birds."

"We have a lot of noisy robins back home. I guess I was a noisy baby, and so my parents decided to name me after those noisy birds."

I nod toward the house. "Do you live here?"

She shrugs. "For now." Again, she looks a little sad. "But hopefully not for much longer."

Oh, that's a bad answer. Anxiety grips me again. She's leaving, and I hardly know who she is. "Where are you going?"

"Well," she says, hesitates and then adds, "I don't know for sure."

I want to ask her so much. I want to tell her about me—all the good stuff anyway, about choir and my plans to solo, and how I'm going to become a paleontologist or a science teacher. But most of all I want to find some cool way to tell her how amazing she is. But I don't say any of that, and for a moment she doesn't say anything either. Then she stands up as if she's going to go, and I start to panic.

"I've been sketching that big osprey circling around the island. That's how I noticed the sheriff's boat and all the activity on the island."

I glance up at the big white and grey bird circling around over the island. I think I noticed it this morning when Toby and I were going out to the island. Now it seems to be watching what is going on. I wonder why it's so interested and what it saw.

Then, out of the blue she says, "So, you want some company on your walk?"

My heart jumps. I open my mouth, but I am completely speechless for a moment. She smiles again, and I say, "Ah . . . that would be great."

"Did you know that, according to Greek mythology, the osprey was named after a king of Athens?" Maude says as we head slowly down the beach.

"Really?" I try to sound interested. "We have them in Washington, but the birds I'm interested in are mostly prehistoric."

"You live in Washington?"

"Yeah, Seattle."

"Is it nice?"

"It's nice, very green, at least around Seattle. My parents think it's the best place in the world. But it's getting kind of crowded, and with the recession, the market for new homes has collapsed."

There's a pause, and I can tell she's a bit confused by my answer.

"And the housing market is important for us because my mom is a mortgage loan officer."

"I see," Maude says, and then picks back up with her story. "Anyway, this king, Pandion, had a son-in-law he couldn't trust, so he turned him into a hawk. Later, a scientist named the genus Pandion. It seems like he should have named it after the king's son-in-law, but he didn't."

"There's a system for naming species called binomial nomenclature," I say, trying to make conversation going. "But figuring out how an animal was originally named can be kinda complicated."

"Well, most people around here call them sea hawks anyway because they only eat fish. But that's just its popular name. A friend of mine who works for Audubon says there isn't really a bird called a sea hawk. What do you call them in Seattle?"

"Just osprey, I think. Our football team is named the Seahawks. But I'm not sure why they picked that name." This isn't my subject, and I feel a little awkward talking about it.

"You're not really interested in birds," says Maude, a note of sarcasm in her voice.

We're making some kind of connection. Maybe this isn't going to be a total disaster if I can just keep talking. "I'm interested in prehistoric birds, mostly. After all, birds evolved from dinosaurs."

"I love birds. They're so perfect. Next to art, they're my favorite things. I belong to this Audubon Society group called BirdWatch. Two or three times a year we do bird counts around the bay."

"Cool," I say. I've heard of those in Seattle, but I'm not exactly sure what they're counting or why. Still I don't want to sound stupid, so I just smile and don't say anything else.

"So, you're interested in dinosaurs?" Maude says finally. "My nephew is interested in dinosaurs, little plastic ones."

We both smile. I realize that Maude is enjoying this, as much as I am. For the first time since we met, I relax enough to tell more about how I became paleontology crazy.

"When I was seven, my parents took me to the American Museum of Natural History. That place is in-credible. They couldn't get me out of the fossil rooms.

I ran from one room to another and then back into the rooms I'd already visited. After that visit, I decided that I wanted to be a paleontologist."

"So you want to spend your life digging up dinosaur bones?"

"Well, not just dinosaur bones but all kind of fossils, and studying them so that we can better understand the evolution of life on Earth."

"Evolution. Now there's a controversial topic."

My heart jumps. Oh no, this could be trouble. "You don't believe in evolution?"

"Yeah, I do big time. But my father's a scientist, and he says evolution is just a theory created by a bunch of atheists to explain the complexity of creation."

I'm dumbstruck. Her father is a scientist who doesn't believe in evolution. How can that be? I start to ask her, but then stop myself. I can see our wonderful first afternoon together ending quickly if I start asking too many questions.

"Yeah, I guess people do have different ideas about that," I say.

There's a pause, as if we're both thinking that it would be best to change the subject. Realizing that I still haven't really learned much about this girl, I nod at her sketchpad and say, "Can I look at your sketches?"

She actually blushes and seems a little hesitant to hand me her sketchbook. "I guess. But they are just sketches, just practice, not really my best work."

I hold out my hand, and she hands me her sketchbook. I flip up the cover, and the black-and-white drawing of an osprey jumps out at me. It seems almost alive. Impressed, I flip through the rest of the book. Some of the drawings are of scenes or buildings. But the ones that have the most energy and that seem the most alive, if not the most realistic, are the human faces and drawings of animals, and especially the birds.

I sigh. "These look pretty good to me."

"They're OK. I just draw for fun, but it's nothing special. I just enjoy it." Then after a pause she adds, "But thanks anyway."

"You like really birds, don't you?"

"They're so beautiful, so self-sufficient and free."

That could be a description of Maude.

Then Maude takes the sketchbook. "So, what do you do for fun, Robin?"

"I sing."

"In a band? My cousin sings in a band called the Noise Machine, which pretty much describes their sound."

"In a choir."

"Wow, how long have you been a singer?"

"Since I was a kid. I don't have a great voice, but I love it. Singing runs in my family, and it always makes me feel happy. I'm hoping I can solo in choir this year."

"That's great," she says.

And I can tell she means it.

"That's the way I feel about my art. I may not be greatest artist. But I love making it, and it's what I want to do. That's how I want to make my living."

I want to tell her more, but it's getting late, and we've wandered far away from Bill's house. A full moon is coming up over the horizon even though it's only dusk. I stop and then she smiles—and it feels like she's reading my mind. I hope that's not the case. We stand looking at the moonlight as it slowly spreads across the bay in the soft, warm twilight. I don't know how long we stand there. By the time we stop, turn, and head back toward our houses, it is almost dark.

The night sky now is beautiful and clear. Despite the moonlight, the stars seem particularly bright. Directly above us is Vega, the brightest star in tonight's sky, and to the east is the Great Square of Pegasus. I point out some of the major stars to Maude. Although I sometimes have trouble getting to the A above middle C, I know my stars and constellations. She seems suitably impressed.

But as beautiful as they are, neither of us is that interested in the sky tonight. Maude seems suddenly distant, lost in her own thoughts. I glance at her and realize again how beautiful she is. And despite, or maybe because of all the stress of the day, I suddenly feel this overpowering urge to kiss her. But maybe she really can read minds because at just that moment she says, "Tell me more about your sister."

Whoosh.

"Robbie, look!"

I know Toby's not there. But in my mind, I see her standing on the shoreline of the island, the little pink camera in her hand. What was she talking about? What did she want me to see? How come I didn't look? As dusk starts to move across the water, Toby's image dissolves, and in its place is the sheriff's patrol boat moving in a wide circle around the little island.

CHAPTER FIVE

Waiting

The big question that remains today is what happened to Toby? Mom grounded me when I got back to the house last night. Now I can't go outside the house unless I'm with one of my parents, and that includes walking on the beach.

I'm still thinking about Maude. Our walk ended kind of abruptly. She wanted to know more about Toby, but I didn't want to tell her any of the details. It would just lead to more questions that I didn't want to answer. Then we were at her steps, and she was gone.

Though she wouldn't give me her telephone number, she said if I came by the steps in the afternoon, she'd "probably" be there sketching, and maybe we could go walking and even stop for a burger.

So far, the investigation has turned up nothing new. The sheriff brought in divers to search around the island this morning. One of the deputies who questioned us the day before came by to tell us that they were looking for a boat that had supposedly passed by the island around noon going north. We stood and watched them from the front porch, nobody saying anything. But I could tell we were all thinking the same thing—Toby might be dead. After a few minutes, I got very anxious and went back up to my room.

Now, from the window in my bedroom, I watch what is happening. I'm so angry. I want to scream out to Mom and everyone else that all this wasn't my fault. But I know nobody will listen. Even the detectives didn't believe it when I told them that I never really had Toby out of my sight after I sat down to listen to my playlist. I was listening to my music and Toby ran off. If she had listened to me and stayed away from the water, none of this would have happened. But nobody will listen to what I have to say.

Again, I'm thinking about what happens to people and things when they disappear. But that's just messing with my head and making me more frustrated. So after a while, I go back and lie down on the bed. Keira and Kelly come into my mind. What are they doing right now? Probably thinking about the start of school. It's our senior year. There will be lots to do besides just classes. I'll have to take the SAT and submit my college applications.

Last spring, I made a list of six colleges that I knew had strong programs in geology or earth sciences. Of course, Yale was on my list. It has the best paleontology program in the country. But it also is out of the question cost-wise and grade-wise. Anyway, as an undergraduate, I'll probably have to major in geology or earth sciences. I hope I'll be able to take some introductory paleontology classes. Berkeley has a great paleontology graduate program, too. It's probably my first choice, but my chances of getting financial aid as an out-of-state student without fantastic grades are pretty slim.

"Be reasonable," Mom says, whenever I start talking about Berkeley.

"You can always transfer to Berkeley after two years if you work hard and keep your grades up," Dad always adds.

I start getting bummed out when I realized how difficult it's going to be to get into a decent school. But Dad's optimism always cheers me up. Of course, there is always the University of Washington, good ol' UW. It has strong geology and earth science programs, and in-state tuition. I just think I'd rather go farther from home. The fallback-option school is Western Washington University in Bellingham.

Dad took me to visit the Western campus this spring, and in June we went to visit Berkeley. That campus is huge! And guess what—they have their own paleontology museum just for students and faculty! Can you imagine what that would be like, having a whole museum full of fossils to study and do research on? I want to go to Berkeley so bad, but I'll have to be patient and work hard this year to get more A's. Then go to someplace like the University of Washington or Western Washington University, and finally transfer to Berkeley my junior year.

Dreaming about the great year ahead makes me feel less stressed. Then there's a knock on my door. It's Bill. He and Mom look a lot alike. Both have broad shoulders and wispy hazel brown hair, except that Bill's hair has some small streaks of grey. But besides looks, the only thing they seem to have in common is music.

"How are you doing, Robin?"

I shrug.

He sits on the edge of the bed. "I know this stuff is tough for you, and it's especially difficult for your parents. They're both really upset."

I don't say anything. I don't want to hear a lecture or get called out as a bad brother.

"I know you're pretty upset too."

"It wasn't my fault!"

"Well, I just wanted to say that if you need to talk about what happened or how you feel about it, I'm here and ready to listen."

"Yeah, sure, but I just . . . What I want . . . What I want is for them—the police I mean—to find Toby and for Mom and Dad to read her the riot act, to ground her for life or whatever. What I want is for everyone to realize it wasn't my fault!"

"Ok," Bill says, "I realize this is difficult for you, but if you need to talk with someone, I'm always here to listen."

I'm not sure what else to say. I wonder if Bill is just doing his minister thing, even though he is supposedly retired. I guess he's had a lot of practice talking with people in trouble.

"And, Robin, you should try talking with your parents, too."

"My parents. They won't listen to me—especially Mom. She thinks I'm a murderer."

"She doesn't think you're a murderer, Robin. She's just having a hard time understanding what's happened."

"I've told them what happened."

I can't tell from Bill's expression exactly what he is thinking. But I have a feeling he doesn't believe me, either. Then he stands up.

"OK, you need some time to think about this. Just remember what I've said."

I like Bill. I'm not really sure why. I didn't really know him before we came on this trip. I've never thought of him as my grandfather, even though he is. He can be kind of distant, but sometimes he surprises me. I still can't figure out how he and Mom can be related.

The day after we arrived, Bill invited his friend Alice over, and they cooked us dinner—salmon, with red potatoes and asparagus from his garden, and Bill's homemade New England chowder. Everything tasted great, and that night I felt right at home. After we ate, Bill got out his guitar and we had a sing-along.

As it turned out, Bill used to be a folk singer. Maybe I shouldn't have been surprised because Mom has a good strong alto voice. I guess even ministers have other lives, although to hear Mom talk, Bill was always busy with his "church work" when she was a kid. So I guess I got the idea that he was kind of a workaholic, without an artistic side.

What I found out was that Bill had played and sung at some clubs and song festivals around New England in the 1960s before he went to divinity school. That was how he met Grandma Helen.

Music, particularly singing, is in our family genes. Take Mom and Dad. They seem like an odd couple. Dad's short and thin, and Mom's tall with broad shoulders. Dad's kind of a thinker. Mom calls him "a dreamer." Anyway, he's slow to react, while Mom is more intense, and a lot more—I guess you'd say—emotional. An outsider might think that their getting together was a case of opposites attracting, but more likely it all had to do with singing because Dad and Mom met while they were both singing in the choir at Commencement Bay College.

At the sing-along, we sang mostly from an old songbook called *Rise Up Singing*, although Bill and Alice, and even Mom, suggested other songs too. Bill had this great old guitar, and Alice played a violin. What I remember now is how good it felt for us all to be together singing. We used to sing together at home when I was a kid. Those were fun times. But that mostly stopped when Mom went back to work.

I hadn't been looking forward to this trip or to being Toby's babysitter. What was I going to do for two weeks in Maine with a grandfather I hardly knew, when all my friends and everything I cared about were in Seattle? But everybody was so relaxed that evening, especially Mom and Dad, that I actually started to feel happy that we had come.

I remember Toby laughing after we'd sung one of those funny songs like "Mrs. Murphy's Chowder" or "James, James." She loves the funny songs. She'll sing them at the top of her voice and then laugh when the song is over. Toby's a funny kid, annoying but still funny. I'm beginning to miss her.

CHAPTER SIX

Burgers and Fries

I've been thinking all afternoon about Maude. Dad and Bill went into town for lunch. Bill asked Mom if I could go with them, but she said no.

"He needs to think about what he has done," Mom said.

Since then Mom has been on the telephone, talking to the state police, to the newspapers, and even to the coordinator of the Obama campaign in Seattle. Right now, she's talking with her boss in Seattle. With her being so preoccupied, I decide to sneak out. Luckily for me, she's using Bill's office to make her calls, and the office door is closed, which means that once I slip down the stairs, I can easily get out the front door.

I must be crazy to try this again! I know Mom's going to be really pissed when she sees I'm gone. But I really want to see Maude again and get away from Mom and all the drama at Bill's. Once the police find Toby, things will settle down. I hope. I just wish they'd hurry up.

I make it out of the house and head down the beach. It takes forever until I reach the four steps leading from the beach up to Maude's house. And sure enough, there's Maude, wearing grey jeans and a purple T-shirt, sitting on the top step. She's just as beautiful as I remember her from yesterday.

"Hi," I say, flashing my biggest and brightest smile—one that says *I'm here and I'm happy to see you, and nothing else matters*—only to stumble over a small rock as I start to jog toward the steps. I don't fall but I stumble, which undercuts my effort to look cool.

"Watch out," Maude says, hardly able to hide her amusement.

When I reach the steps, Maude is leaning back, her hands behind her, her arms holding her up. The sketch pad is sitting beside her. At first, neither of us seem to know what to say.

"Been here long?" I ask finally, an awkward attempt to get a conversation going.

"About an hour."

"Get any drawing done?"

"Some," she says with a sigh.

Before I can ask what she's been working on, Maude asks about Toby. "Have they found your sister?"

"No," I say, already feeling anxious.

I'd been thinking about how I was going to handle this question on my walk from Bill's. I had a plan—tell her as little as possible and then find a way to change the subject. But now that the subject had come up, my mind freezes.

"You want to walk?" Maude asks.

"Yeah," I say.

It's a good afternoon for walking. The sky is again deep blue, and the sun is summer-bright. There is a little on-shore breeze. It reminds me of the breeze yesterday, the one I felt just before Toby disappeared, but it's not nearly so hot.

Maude smiles and then stands up. Then, without a word, she starts off down the beach. This takes me by surprise, and I have to pick up my pace to catch up with her. For a few minutes, neither of us say anything.

"So what happened?" she asks finally.

"We're not sure. The sheriff hasn't found any trace of her."

"She was out on the island and just didn't come back?"

"Well, sort of." I hesitate and then add, "Actually, we were both out on the island. I sat down to listen to some music on my MP3, and after a few minutes, when I didn't hear her, I got up and she was gone."

The expression on Maude's face changes, and I can see the questions going through her mind. "I know it sounds crazy, but that's what happened. One minute Toby was there, and the next minute she was gone."

"God, that's awful! You must have been really upset when you couldn't find her."

"Yeah, I was. I went crazy, running around the island looking for her." I want to tell her every detail of that afternoon on the island, and I might have, too, except that she breaks in and asks another question.

"I bet your parents are really upset."

"Oh, my parents are upset, alright." But I don't want to talk about my parents. I want to talk about me. "Yeah, it's really upsetting. We're just hoping the police find her soon." Then, before she can ask any more questions about Toby, I change the subject. "So tell me about you."

She smiles. It's an uncomfortable smile. And I remember how uncomfortable she seemed to be in talking about herself yesterday. "Like what?"

"Like, what school do you go to?"

"Belfast High, of course."

"I should have known," I say with a smile. And with that, the atmosphere gets lighter. "You're a senior?"

"Going to be a senior," Maude says. "It's my last year at Bell's—that's what everybody calls it—and hopefully my last year here."

"But you're not counting the days," I say sarcastically.

"Oh, yes, I am."

"You're going to college?"

"Yeah, and I've even got a college picked out."

"Where?"

"The Rhode Island School of Design."

"That's in Rhode Island?" I feel silly the moment I ask the question, but Maude just smiles, and I realize that once again we're connecting.

"You've got it, mister. The Rhode Island School of Design in Providence. It's two hundred sixty-five miles southwest of Belfast, and a million miles away in terms of everything that's important."

"What about you?'

"Hopefully, I'm going to Berkeley."

"Oh," Maude says, "aiming high."

"Yeah, but if not, I'll go to either the University of Washington or Western."

"So you've got a backup plan."

"Realistically, I guess I have to have one. And like Dad says, no matter where I get accepted, if my grades are good enough, I can always transfer after the first two years."

"Your high school grades aren't great?"

"I struggled the first year. French killed me. I have no facility for languages, and the teacher was only interested in grammar."

Maude smiles. "*Je ne parle pas français*?"

"Oh, great. She's fluent in French."

We both laugh, and I suddenly feel very hungry. "Hey, you said something about getting a burger yesterday."

"Hungry, huh?"

"Yeah, I only had a banana and cup of coffee for breakfast."

"The Bay Burger Shack is over the hill on the highway," Maude says.

I check my wallet and find one $5 bill and some change. Hopefully that's enough to get a burger and something to drink.

"Let's go."

Well, the Bay Burger Shack is a little further than just over the hill. But it turns out to be a nice walk along a side road that runs from the highway to the beach. The restaurant is one of those local drive-in places that looks like it was built in the 1960s. It is small—just a counter and a waiting area inside. Outside, there is a long strip of covered parking where people, mostly teenagers, can sit in their cars and eat. On the other side of the building, there are some tables in a little grove of trees. A big speaker blares out oldies rock music into the car park. Fortunately, the outside sitting area is fairly quiet and much less crowded.

We both get the Shack's "world famous fish 'n' chips," along with diet cokes. Maude doesn't eat red meat. And who am I to argue with such beauty? So I get the same thing. After all, why bring up a tricky subject—like the fact that I am a committed carnivore—when we're just starting to get to know each other?

Since I'm a little short of cash, I get the kid's meal version of the fish 'n' chips. Maude laughs when I order, and she can't help smiling again after we sit down to eat at one of the outside tables. I have to admit, it's pretty funny watching me try to make a meal out of one piece of fish and ten fries. I cut my French fries in half to make the meal seem bigger and drink out of a plastic kid's cup, which is covered with animal decals.

Anyway, Maude doesn't ask me if I'm broke or just cheap, and she also doesn't offer to pay—that would really be embarrassing. But she does sort of turn up her nose when I smother everything with catsup.

"So, what's your backup plan if you can't get into the design school?" I ask.

"I don't have one," she says casually, as she picks apart a piece of fish with her fork.

"That's gutsy. You must be pretty confident that you'll get accepted."

"Well, I've got a 3.85 GPA, and I've been president of both the Art Club and the Math Club. I think it will all come down to how well they like my portfolio."

"Are those the sketches you've been working on the last couple days?"

"No, those were just for fun. An artist friend of mine let me use her studio some this summer. That's where I put together my portfolio. I'll mail out everything for early admission—the application and portfolio—next week."

"What about your SATs?"

"I took those in the spring."

This girl is beautiful and smart, too.

"Pretty cool. So now you can start making plans for your college career."

Maude shrugs. "So now I start planning for the most important art project of my life."

I wait for her to continue while she finishes a fry.

"Applying is only the beginning of the process. About two-thirds of the applicants don't make the first cut. Those that are left are invited to campus in the fall to demonstrate their skills. That means that you go to Providence for four days. You spend the first two creating an art project from scratch in one of the school's studios. Then you meet some of the faculty and a few older students. And finally you are interviewed by the acceptance team."

"Wow, that could be tense."

"Oh, it could be fun," Maude says. "I just hope I get invited."

"But what about you?" Maude asks after we've spent a couple of minutes finishing our food. "Why do you want to go to Berkeley? Doesn't the University of Washington have a good geology program?"

"It does, and I should probably be focused on getting in there. It's just that Berkeley has such a great paleontology graduate program." I pause and then add, "And my Dad has a bit of bad history with UW. I don't think his problems would hurt my getting accepted, but I feel like he'd rather I went to either Western or Berkeley."

Maude's eyebrows rise. "So what happened?"

"Oh, he was in the Astronomy Department, and he didn't get tenure."

She shrugs and then asks, "What's so special about Berkeley?"

"They have the best paleontology museum of any university in the country, and it's all for the use of faculty and students. Can you imagine what it would be like to be a student studying paleontology at Berkeley?"

"I don't know Robin, you look more like a singer to me than you do a dinosaur hunter."

She's kidding me. I can tell. But I take the remark as a compliment. "That's because you come from a family that questions evolution."

"Actually, I don't question evolution. It's my Dad who questions it."

"And how can someone who calls himself a scientist question evolution?"

As I'm looking across the table at Maude and waiting for an answer, my heart jumps. Over her shoulder, I see Mom and Dad walking toward us from inside the restaurant. "Shit!"

Maude tenses. "What's the matter?"

"Hello, Robin," Dad says, before I can explain or even warn Maude that my parents have arrived.

My eyes fix on Mom. She looks like she's ready to kill me. Dad's calmer, but I can tell he's not happy either. I manage to rather sloppily introduce Maude to my parents.

She smiles warmly and extends her hand to Dad. "Nice to meet you, Mr. Steele."

Dad responds with a forced smile and a thank you.

Then she turns and extends her hand to Mom, who takes it, but just nods.

"We were just talking about college," I say, as if that will answer all my parents' questions about why I snuck off when I was supposed to stay at Bill's.

I glance at Dad. I can tell he's trying to decide how to handle the situation, now that he knows someone else is involved, even peripherally, in my Maine world.

But then Mom wades right in to make things sound as bad as possible. "You see, Maude, our daughter is missing."

"Yes, Robin told me. How terrible. I just hope she is OK."

Mom seems a little taken aback by the sincerity of Maude's response.

"Thank you, but as I was saying, we were all waiting at Robin's grandfather's house—he's Bill Saunders. Maybe you know him?"

Maude shakes her head. Is that a yes or no?

Mom doesn't wait for a real answer. She says, "We were waiting in case the police called with any news about Toby. All of us were supposed to stay around, and then Robin just disappeared. So you can imagine how we felt when we couldn't find him. One child missing and then a day later, another one gone."

"Yes," Maude says quietly. I can tell by her body language that all the good feelings from our walk on the beach are disappearing. Mom's poison is starting to do its work. I can tell Maud's going to leave.

"Nice to meet you," she tells my parents, trying to sound as upbeat as possible. "I'm sorry it couldn't have been under happier circumstances, but I'll be praying that you find Toby safe."

Then she turns to me. To my surprise, she squeezes my hand and smiles weakly. It isn't the bright, mischievous smile I saw flashes of over the last two days, the one that drove me crazy and made me want so badly to be with her. No, it is the tired, melancholy smile I glimpsed that first moment I saw her sitting on the steps with her sketchpad. It is as if she is saying—*Oh, Robin Steele, it was nice to meet you. Sorry you're having trouble, but I've got troubles too, and no time to deal with any more*. Then, she turns and walks away from our table and back toward the beach. The way things are going, I wonder if I will ever see her again.

CHAPTER SEVEN

Something Found

I am totally grounded after the Bay Burger Shack incident. I don't know what my parents are most unhappy about: the fact that I left the house, or that I was
hanging out with a girl and having a little fun when I
should have been wearing black and moping around
the house. So now I'm supposed to report to either
Mom or Dad once an hour until they're convinced I'm
not going to run off. That's just how Mom put it.

"We can't have you running off. I know you'd like to
treat Toby's disappearance as if it never happened.
But you can't. We won't let you."

"Robin, right now you need to stay with the family,"
Dad added when I protested that I couldn't stand being cooped up in the house for who knows how long.

I could hardly stand getting out of bed this morning. When I got downstairs, Dad suggested that we all
go to church. Thinking it would get me out of the house,
I agreed to go, but nobody else, not even Bill, seemed
interested.

"I can't attend my old church until January," he said.
It's a Unitarian rule; a retired minister can't return to
his old church for two years. We could drive to Portland,
but I don't think we'd make it in time for the service."

Instead, Bill made us a big breakfast: pancakes, eggs, veggie sausage—the works. Both of my parents are pseudo-vegetarians. They don't eat red meat or chicken, but they do eat fish and some dairy. Lucky for me, the benevolence fairy touched them with her wand when I was pretty young and told them not to force their eating habits on their kids. So they never told me I can't eat meat. But—and this is the catch 22—they never cook meat or chicken at home. Instead it's tofu-this, eggplant-that, and fish twice a week. So besides lunch at school, the only red meat I get is if I fix myself a burger on the weekends or get invited over to Mike's for dinner. His dad loves to grill steaks.

Toby, on the other hand, is well on her way to becoming a food radical. Last year, she started a petition asking her school to buy only organic food for the school cafeteria. Then she refused to eat chicken after she got to know the chickens being raised by our next-door neighbor. But the pinnacle of Toby's activism was the tater tot boycott.

Tater tots are a staple of school lunches. Everybody knows they are junk food, but kids, especially elementary school kids, love them. Anyway, Toby recruited a few of her friends. The group made signs, and one day when the school menu included tater tots, Toby's guerrillas—all four of them—descended on the lunchroom to start the boycott. School cafeterias at lunchtime are one of the busiest and noisiest places in any school. The lines are long, the kids are hungry, and everybody is talking. When Toby and her gang tried to block one of the lunch lines to talk to other kids about the evils of tater tots, it turned into a big mess. A few kids agreed with Toby, and her shock troops swelled to about ten. But most of the kids just wanted to eat. There was a little yelling, and some kids tried to push past the boycott line. A girl trying to juggle a food tray fell, and within minutes, Mr. Mercer, the assistant principal, showed up to escort the agitators off to his office.

Dad came to the school, apologized to the VP, and took Toby home for the day. That night, he talked to everybody about what had happened and what we could learn from the incident, while Mom just sat back and listened. I remember thinking, *Mom is never this quiet, and she certainly would have a lot to say if I pulled a stunt like that.* As it turned out, the other agitators suffered more than Toby, even though she was the instigator. As a punishment, Sally Biggs, Toby's best friend, couldn't go anywhere but to school for two weeks.

Bill's breakfast turns out great, but nobody except me seems very hungry. Bill takes some eggs and a piece of toast. Dad has one pancake and a piece of the veggie sausage, and Mom drinks coffee and eats a piece of toast. But I load up my plate up with food, and just as I'm starting to dig in, I realize that both Mom and Dad are staring at me again. By now, Mom is on her second cup of coffee, and I can tell by the look in her eyes that she's thinking, *How can he enjoy food when Toby is missing?*

Well, I don't care. They can't stop me from eating. I take two big bites of eggs, get about a half a pancake down, and then the telephone rings. It's the sheriff's office. They've found something on the beach, and they want to bring it by to see if we can identify it.

About twenty minutes later, a red-headed deputy shows up at the front door. I vaguely recognize him as one of the deputies who was here the day Toby disappeared. That afternoon is still a bit of a blur to me.

He introduces himself again as Deputy Murphy. Bill asks him in to join the four of us in the kitchen. He's carrying a plastic police evidence bag, and after he sits down, he takes a little pink camera out of the bag. Mom gives an audible sigh. You can clearly see the funny little cat face on the front of the camera. It's Toby's, alright.

"Where did you find it?" Dad asks.

"Actually, a girl found it while she was walking home along the bay yesterday evening."

"Where?"

"About a half mile south of here. She found it lodged behind a small bunch of rocks. The beach narrows along that stretch of the bay. It could have been brought in by the previous high tide and deposited in the rocks."

"Is that what you think happened?" Dad asks.

Officer Murphy shrugs. "That's what seems most likely."

All this time Mom has been just staring at the camera. Now she looks over at Officer Murphy. "But you don't know that for sure," she says.

"No, not for sure," Officer Murphy says, after a short pause. "But it looks like the camera was in the water at some point."

Mom reaches out her hand. It's clear she wants to touch the camera, but Murphy pulls the camera out of her reach.

"I'm sorry, Mrs. Steele. I can't let you touch the camera. After I leave here, I'm taking it up to Augusta. They'll check it for prints and for DNA. I can't let any of you handle it until that is done."

This clearly irritates Mom. "This couldn't have just been dropped on the beach?" she asks.

Officer Murphy tilts his head as if he's thinking about exactly how to respond. "Hard to say—but we'll know more after we get the camera examined. For now, two officers will be working their way south from where the camera was found, looking for more information on the little girl."

Mom bristles. "Toby. Her name is Toby."

"Yes, *Toby*," Officer Murphy says and stands up. "But before I go, I need something more of Toby's, so we can check her DNA. Do you have a comb or a hairbrush that she used regularly?"

"Yes, a hairbrush," Mom responds.

"OK, could you get it please."

Mom gets up and leaves the room.

There's a pause while the three of us sit looking at each other, and I start to fidget nervously. Then, Dad gets up to get another cup of coffee. He offers one to Officer Murphy, who shakes his head.

"It just gives me the jitters."

As he is sitting back down, Dad asks, "Who was the girl?"

"The girl?"

"The one who found the camera."

"Oh, the MacAndrews girl. She lives with her father just down the beach. She . . ."

"That's the girl we met last night," Dad says before Murphy can finish his sentence. He looks over at me, as if he expects me to say something.

Maude found Toby's camera? I can't believe it. I look down at my food but say nothing. I'm not hungry anymore.

Just then Mom returns to the kitchen, Toby's hairbrush in hand. Apparently, she heard the last part of the conversation.

"What do you know about this?" Mom asks me bluntly.

"Nothing."

Mom might have blown up at me again if it hadn't been for Dad asking Deputy Murphy if they have any more information about the boat that was seen near the island when Toby disappeared.

"Nothing significant," the deputy says. "It's moored off Bar Harbor, but no one was on board. We're assuming they're in town or visiting the national park."

That ends the conversation. I'm thinking of Maude again and wondering if she had any idea that the camera she found on the beach was Toby's. Officer Murphy excuses himself and leaves.

"I know the MacAndrews," says Bill, after Officer Murphy leaves. "Their family has lived on the bay for generations. Claude—that's the father—calls himself a scientist and teaches at the evangelical college in Bangor."

"Claude MacAndrews," the name bursts out of Dad's mouth. "I know that name. I think he was one of those so-called scientists who wrote a paper for the Bush administration questioning the importance of human activity on climate change."

"Yes," says Bill, "he's an interesting fellow. The last year I was at the church, I attended a conference of the Maine Council of Churches in Portland, where we discussed what role Maine churches should take in discussions about climate change. Most of the churches in attendance were supporting an effort to pass a broad carbon tax. But Claude showed up with a letter from a few of the more conservative churches and argued that we needed to look very closely at the economic effects before we supported any large-scale green initiative. Of course, he also argued that the evidence of a substantial human impact was still in question."

So, Maude's father is a denier. I wonder how it feels to live with a father like that, particularly for someone like Maude, who seems so smart. I can see why she wants to move out.

"Apparently, he has a degree in chemistry from some small college in the Midwest. I run into him now and then when I'm taking my morning walk on the beach, and he usually tries to engage me in conversation. I think he's trying to convert me. I don't think he sees Unitarianism as being a real religion."

"That must be irritating," says Dad.

"Oh," Bill says and smiles. "I kind of enjoy it. He seems to know enough about science to make a cogent argument, and it also gives me a chance to challenge his ideas."

"Do you know the daughter very well?" Mom asks.

"Not well." Then he nods toward me and adds, "But I like what I've seen, and I hear she's smart—president of the high school math club and last year editor of the school newspaper."

"She's an artist, too," I say quietly. Mom glares at me, and I stop talking. Still I wonder what happened to Maude's mother and if she was more understanding than my mom.

"So now I guess we wait," Dad says.

"I can't stand it," Mom blurts out in a shrill voice. "The waiting, the not knowing!" She walks over to the kitchen window and looks out.

"We have to do something. The sheriff is taking too long."

Dad looks disturbed. "What else can we do?" he asks quietly.

There is a long pause and finally Mom answers. "I think we should make some signs with Bill's telephone number on them and then post them everywhere, in town and along the beach. We can put them in people's mailboxes. I've already talked to the area newspapers, but most are weeklies, and I'm not sure how many people actually read them. Then, I want to look online to see if there is a website where we can post information about Toby's disappearance."

Finally, she turns back from the window and looks straight at me. "And I want to talk with this girl, Robin! The one who found Toby's camera. I want to see if she knows anything that she didn't tell the police."

"Why?" I blurt out.

"Because, as of now, she is the only lead we have."

My heart sinks. I can see Mom interrogating Maude and making a fool of herself and me in the process. This is going to be such a disaster.

CHAPTER EIGHT

A Call from Home

There is no word from the sheriff's office by Monday morning. Dad says it's probably too early. But Mom is getting more and more impatient. Myself, I'm starting to wonder if we'll ever see Toby again. That thought scares me, so I quickly push it out of my mind.

Just to be doing something, Mom marshals the three of us to follow through on her plan to flood the area with flyers about Toby. As it turns out, Bill's old computer has Print Shop, a software program that makes it possible for Mom to create a flyer in about thirty minutes. Dad and I volunteer to take the flyer to the local copy shop to print and then start distributing the flyers around town. Right now, I'll do anything to get out of this house and away from Mom. Maybe helping out a bit with Mom's crazy plan will get her off my back for a while.

Bill suggests that he go by the McAndrews' place later in the day to talk with Maude, while Mom stays at the house to search for websites where she can post information about Toby's disappearance.

Dad and I head downtown. Downtown Belfast is built in a triangle along Main and Church streets. Apparently, a lot of the buildings are very old. Bill said there is a whole block downtown, the Hayford Block, which is on some kind of historical register. Most of the buildings along the triangle have been restored and are occupied by antique stores or boutiques.

We make our way along Main, posting flyers in the stores that will let us, which aren't very many. Then we turn onto Church Street. Just past a beautiful old building called the Belfast Opera House, we come to a bookstore, Bay Books. Thinking the bookstore is likely to have a bulletin board, we go inside. Like a lot of businesses in Belfast, Bay Books is full of what Dad calls "period furniture." I can see the attraction for older people and tourists, but it doesn't look very comfortable to me.

On one side of the bookstore, behind a big wooden stand-up information desk, there is a girl or young woman standing with her back us. She looks vaguely familiar. Then she turns around and I realize why. It's Maude!

"Maude," I say in surprise.

Maude looks up from whatever she is doing. She doesn't smile, or frown, so I can't tell if she's surprised or even interested to see me.

When he realizes who she is, Dad strides up to the desk. "Hi, Ms. McAndrews," he says. "We met last night at that burger place."

"Yes, Mr. Steele," she says, "I remember you." She still doesn't smile, and she doesn't even acknowledge me. And me, I just stand there behind Dad, feeling stupid.

"What can I do for you?" Maude asks.

"Robin and I are posting flyers about Toby's disappearance, and we wondered if we might post one in your store?"

Dad hands her a flyer.

"We're only supposed to post items that have to do with the bookstore—you know, notices about author readings and things like that," Maude replies. She nods toward a small corkboard on the back wall next to a door marked *Office*. "As you can see, the board is basically full."

She's right, the wallboard is filled with postings.

There is a long pause. I know what I'd like to say—I want to tell her how sorry I am that my parents barged in on us at the Burger Shack and made such a scene. That's what I want to say, and then I'd like to ask her about finding Toby's camera. But I just stand there in front of the bookstore information desk and say nothing.

But Dad keeps talking, "Could we leave a few of the flyers for you to keep here at the information desk?"

Maude looks at the flyer and asks, "Are the police having any luck in their search for Toby?"

"Not yet. The one lead was your finding Toby's camera on the beach," Dad replies. "And thanks, we really appreciate your picking it up and calling the sheriff."

Maude smiles, a slight, self-conscious smile. "So that was your daughter's camera. I'm glad I could help." Then that thought or something else registers with Maude. "Let me talk with Mrs. Henderson. She's the owner." She turns toward me. "I'd like to do whatever I can to help if I can."

"That's great," Dad says, and without pausing asks, "We were wondering if you could tell us if there was anything you noticed when you found the camera that, you know, that you may not have told the sheriff?"

"No, not really. Like I told the deputy, I was walking home from the Burger Shack. I came to a place where the beach practically disappears, and I had to walk around some rocks. And as I did, I noticed something pink behind the biggest rock."

"So you picked it up?"

"No, when I saw it was a camera, I bent down to take a closer look and noticed that it was probably a child's camera, so I called the sheriff. I was afraid no one would come out on a Saturday night, but a deputy showed up in about ten minutes. I gave him a statement and he took the camera."

"Was the camera wet?"

"At first, I didn't think so. But one side looked wet when the deputy picked it up."

"Did you notice anything else lying around, anything that might have belonged to a little girl?"

"No."

Dad nods, and I can tell from the look on his face that he's thinking, *this doesn't help us much.*

"Thanks," he says to Maude.

She smiles at him and then turns and smiles at me.

Now it's my turn to smile. "Thanks, Maude," I say, but before I can say more, Dad shepherds me out of the store.

After leaving the bookstore, we finish handing out flyers along Church Street. Fewer than half of the stores will even take one, though as we walk back past the bookstore, I notice that one has been taped to the front door. I search the big bookstore window as we walk by for any sign of Maude, but I don't see her anywhere. An older woman with grey hair is now at the information desk. As we leave the downtown area, we post a flyer outside the town hall and leave one more at a convenience store right across the street from where Dad has parked the car.

When we get home, Mom is on the telephone with someone, and she sounds upset. I can't really make out what she is talking about, but I start feeling ice cold again. This has got to be bad news. Dad and I look at each other. We are both thinking the same thing. The call is from the sheriff, and it's about Toby.

After a minute, Bill comes in from the back yard. Through the window I notice his friend Alice working in the garden. He looks at both of us, and the first thing he says is, "It's a call from her boss in Seattle."

"Nothing from the sheriff?" Dad asks.

"No," says Bill.

Dad gets a cup of coffee, and I grab some juice. We're all sitting in the kitchen when I suddenly realize that I'm not hearing Mom talking on the phone. I brace myself, and a minute or two later Mom comes into the kitchen. If anything, she looks even more upset than when we left this morning.

"What's going on, Claire?" Dad asks.

"That was Dan."

Dan Baker is her office manager. Her company's motto is, "We sell the American Dream." Once I heard Mom and Dad talking about her job, and she mentioned Dan and how much he wanted salespeople to use the motto as much as possible. Dad seemed to find that kinda funny.

"We're having an all-office meeting on Wednesday morning. Everybody has to be there, no exceptions."

"Did you tell Dan that we still haven't found Toby?"

"Yes," Mom says, her voice rising as she lets Dad know she doesn't appreciate such a stupid question.

"And what did he say?" Dad asks, ignoring Mom's obvious irritation.

"He apologized but stressed that everybody has to be at this meeting. If I don't show up, he'll have to let me go."

"What's this meeting about?" Dad asks.

There is another long silence. I think everyone is in shock. But I'm thinking, *What does this mean for me*?

Then Mom says, "So it's nonnegotiable. I have to fly home tomorrow, and I have to make plane reservations as soon as I can." She looks straight at Dad and adds, "So you and I need to talk, and then I need to call and make my reservations."

They go upstairs to talk in the bedroom while Bill and I stay in the kitchen.

"Any luck handing out those flyers?" Bill asks.

"Only about half of the places would take them."

"I'm surprised you got that many. Tourism and retirement are big business in Belfast. And the downtown businesses like to convey the image of the town as an old-fashioned and safe community."

"The big surprise was that we ran into Maude."

"Where?"

"She works at the bookstore. It must be a summer job."

"So how did that go?"

"I felt so stupid about Mom and Dad giving us the third degree at the Burger Shack on Saturday that I was too embarrassed to say anything. Anyway, Dad did most of the talking, and Maude apparently doesn't know any more than what the deputy told us about finding Toby's camera."

"Oh, that's too bad. I'm not surprised though." He pauses for a minute and then adds, "But maybe you'll see her again."

"I've got to. I need to apologize for my parents, and I've got to show her that I'm not just a stupid jerk who put his little sister's life in danger. I'll sneak out of the house again to see her if I have to."

Bill sighs. "That's probably not a great idea. Maybe we can work it out so you and I can visit the MacAndrews after Claire leaves."

"Do you think she'll go home without Dad and me?"

"Someone will have to stay here to be in direct contact with the sheriff. Anyway, let's stay positive and see what happens."

Suddenly, I see some hope in what has seemed hopeless. Dad and I will stay here to continue looking for Toby. Mom will go home, and before she comes back, I'll get to see Maude again. Who knows, maybe when Mom returns, they'll have found Toby, and this whole nightmare will all be over. My optimism lasts for about thirty minutes. After talking in private, Mom and Dad come back down to the kitchen. Neither of them looks happy.

Bill was half right. Dad will stay in Belfast, keeping in contact with the sheriff and state police. He's not scheduled to teach at the community college until the last week in September, so he is the obvious person to stay. But my vacation is over. I'm going back to Seattle with Mom almost a week early, where I'm sure I'll be grounded until school starts. I can't believe it. This can't be happening! I stand up and sit back down again. Finally, I can't keep it in any longer.

"I want to see Maude before I leave."

"You need to be here to help your mom get ready to leave," Dad says immediately.

And before I can say anything else, Mom adds, "This is no longer a vacation, Robin. This is a family crisis, and with your attitude, you've shown that you're not interested in accepting any responsibility or even in really helping find your sister."

"That's not true," I retort, but I can tell by her face and body language that Mom doesn't care what I say.

"You're coming home with me, mister. You're just in the way here. Maybe when you get home, you'll have some time to think about what you have done, along with getting ready for school."

I glance over at Dad to see if he might help me plead my case. He stands sternly just behind Mom, and I know that I'm not going to get any help from him.

The decision has been made. I'm going home without Toby and without being able to see Maude again to tell her I'm sorry. I want to scream *This is so unfair*! but even that wouldn't do any good.

And there's no appeal to this decision.

CHAPTER NINE

Responsibility

Bill hastily organizes a going-away dinner for Mom and me Monday evening. Mom spends the rest of the afternoon making the plane reservations, talking with Dad, and starting to pack. By dinnertime, she is getting more and more frantic.

Dinner is a simple affair. Bill makes pasta and cooks some beans grown in his backyard garden. Alice joins us and brings a big green salad. She reminds me of one of those mothers you see in old television shows, kind of pretty, but also a little tired looking. She's always practically dressed and likes to spend a lot of her time in the kitchen and the garden.

The idea of a group dinner probably sounded good when Bill first thought about it. Now everybody's stressed. I know I haven't really slept much for three nights. Dinnertime could have been a chance for all of us to just relax. But with the way things are, with Mom and me sitting at the same table, there is likely to be trouble. I can feel a blowup coming the moment I sit down.

Once everybody starts eating, Alice asks Mom about our travel plans. Turns out we'll be catching a 1:30 p.m. flight out of Portland, stopping in Chicago, and getting into Seattle at 10:00 p.m.

When Alice asks me if I am looking forward to going home, I shrug and say, "Not really."

And before anyone else can jump in—meaning Mom—I add that I'd rather stay and help look for Toby. That's all it takes for Mom to get fired up.

"Actually, Robin's interest in this girl he's met has become a distraction. That's why we thought it was best that he go home with me."

Immediately, I want to defend myself. But out of the corner of my eye I see Bill look over at Dad, and before I can say anything, Dad does.

"We both think Robin and his mom need to have some quality time together. They're—we're going through a very tough time right now, and it seems to have been the most difficult for them."

Both Mom and I look at Dad.

Quality time! What is Dad talking about? They might just as well shoot me in the head and save the money on the plane flight. I drop my fork on my plate, stand up, and start to leave. I want to get away from Mom and Dad and everybody as quickly as I can—but no such luck. Mom immediately commands me to sit back down.

After that, the dinner goes on in almost complete silence. We just eat our food, and try to pretend that everything is just great with the Steele family, and that Mom and I will spend our time on the flight home singing and holding hands. Can I even picture that in my head? No, I can't!

Finally, Bill asks Mom if she is concerned about being called home so abruptly. At first, Mom frowns and tries to ignore the question. But with everybody waiting for an answer, she finally has to say something.

"These are tough times for mortgage lenders. Home sales are way down. In fact, our company, American

Dream, may have to do some cutting back. But I don't think it will affect me, except that I might have to take on more work."

Dad rolls his eyes when he hears this.

Mom sees him and frowns. "I'll know more after I get back," she adds.

When everyone finishes eating, Bill makes his own announcement. With Alice's help, he is going to turn his quarter-acre backyard into an organic garden, with most of the produce going to a local food bank.

"That's a great idea," Dad says.

Alice smiles. "This area really needs more local food going to the food backs. Most of what they get now is surplus food from restaurants and stores, mostly canned stuff and leftovers. A lot of people here are struggling to just get by."

You can tell Alice is excited about the idea. But Mom has other things on her mind. She frowns and looks at the kitchen clock, and our big going-home dinner feels over.

It's late evening now, but even after reading half a book I brought from Seattle, I can't sleep. So I head downstairs to get a glass of milk. While I'm in the kitchen, I hear soft singing coming from Bill's small office. I slowly push the door open. Bill and Mom are singing. It's one of those sad folk ballads, about death and regret. Mom looks really sad, but the moment she sees me, her body tenses and she stops singing.

"Go back to bed, Robin. We've got a busy day tomorrow."

Bill smiles at me, as if to say he wishes I could come in and join them, but that's not going to happen. I get my glass of milk, and go back to my room. I still can't sleep. The clock in the kitchen had said 1:00 a.m. It's already Tuesday. *How can I face this day*?

After I don't know how long, I hear Mom coming up the stairs.

The sun is flooding into my room when I wake up. But I can't manage to get out of bed until Dad knocks on my door. Then I fumble around, take a shower, get dressed, and finally start to pack. I don't want to go downstairs. I can't face the prospect of flying home alone with Mom.

My stomach is growling and I've got a headache, but I trudge down to the kitchen. Maybe it won't be so bad to leave, I say to myself. Maine has become a constant reminder of Toby. Once I get back to Seattle, things will be more normal if I can just survive the flight home with Mom. Maybe by then they will have found Toby.

Still I can't stand the thought that I may never see Maude again.

Dad and Bill are sitting in the kitchen, drinking coffee and talking softly. They get noticeably quieter when I walk in. I pour some cereal in a bowl, get a glass of orange juice, and I'm just sitting down to eat when there is a knock at the front door. Bill goes to the door and returns with Deputy Murphy, who is carrying a large envelope.

"Is Mrs. Steele here?" he asks.

"I'll go get her," Dad says and he leaves the room.

After a minute, Mom appears. She is dressed like she's ready to go, but she looks exhausted. There are big grey bags under her eyes, and she keeps blinking them like the light is bothering her.

"OK," says Murphy. "I want to update you on a couple things. Let's have everybody sit down. "First, we did find the people on the boat that I mentioned to you the last time we talked."

There's a pause. Everybody is staring at Murphy now.

"The boat belongs to a lawyer from Connecticut. He and his family were going up the coast on Friday, and they passed through this area of the bay around noon. But he wasn't sure of the exact time. And nobody on the boat remembers seeing anyone on the island, or even the island itself for that matter."

"I can't believe that," Mom says.

"Well, that's what they say, and we have no reason to dispute what they're saying, at least right now."

I can tell Mom isn't satisfied with the deputy's answer, and even Dad looks skeptical.

"So where does that leave us?" he asks Deputy Murphy.

"Well, the lawyer did say something that might give us a clue about what happened."

"What?" Dad asks.

"He said that while they were traveling north in the bay, they ran into a big wave that actually shook their boat. Again, he doesn't remember exactly where they were at the time, but he does remember that it was before they got to Belfast."

Dad and Mom look at each other.

"So it could have been a rip tide?" Bill asks.

"Probably a rogue wave," says the deputy. "But, so far, no one at the Belfast marina seems to remember seeing or feeling such a wave."

I don't think this was the news any of us wanted to hear. I wait for Dad or Mom to ask more questions. But everyone just sits at the kitchen table looking at Deputy Murphy, or staring at the table.

"Well, let's move on," he says after a moment. "We had one of our people in Bangor working on this all day Monday. She found a partial fingerprint on the camera that was Toby's. She compared it with one she found on Toby's hairbrush. There is only some trace DNA, nothing conclusive. But through some kind of wizardry, she was able to get one picture off the camera."

"You got a picture off Toby's camera after it had been in the water?" Dad asks.

"Yes sir," says Officer Murphy. "It's a digital camera, and I guess sometimes now with the new technology they can save pictures."

He hands the envelope to Dad, who pulls out the picture, looks at it, and sighs deeply. Then he quickly puts it back into the envelope and, instead of handing it to Mom, he hands it to me.

My hand is shaking as I reach into the envelope and take out the picture. What if it shows Toby's body? I hesitate, and then pull out the picture. It is blurry and lopsided, and at first, I can't make out much of anything. Then I realize it's a view from the east side of the island looking west toward the small tree where we had spread out our towels. That means it was taken either from the water's edge or from the water. I can make out the little tree, and right below it someone is lying on the ground. It's me, and it is pretty obvious that I am sleeping.

"Give me the picture, Robin," Mom says.

I look up from the picture and look over at Mom. My hand is shaking again, and I drop the picture on the floor. Dad picks it up and hands it to Mom.

She looks at the picture and then she looks at me. I can see the anger on her face and my heart starts to pound. "I just can't believe this. Of all the irresponsible things you've done, Robin, this is the worst."

"This isn't my fault," I protest.

"I can't hear any more of this," she says. "Go to your room and get your stuff packed. We're leaving in an hour."

That's it. There's no way I can appeal to stay longer now. Not even Deputy Murphy seems shocked by my mom's outburst. Everybody is angry and upset and, apparently, everybody agrees that Toby's disappearance is my fault.

I must look pretty upset myself because Bill offers to take me upstairs to help me pack. "Sit down on the bed and take a deep breath," he says, when we get to my room. Slowly, my breathing returns to normal and my heart slows down.

"I wish Mom would get off my case. She's just making things worse."

Bill sits down beside me and sighs. "I can't say how you should feel right now, Robin. But you need to talk to your mother and to try and understand how she is feeling."

"Talk to Mom! She won't listen to me. She doesn't care what I have to say."

There's a pause, and then Bill says, "I know it seems like Claire is being pretty hard on you, but Toby disappeared when you and she were alone on that island. When you were supposed to be watching her. Right now, Claire is scared and she's angry and she's focused on blaming you."

"I've told everybody what happened. After we got there, Toby started wandering around with that little camera of hers, and I told her not to go in the water and to stay where I could see her. The next thing I knew, she was gone."

"Is that all?"

"I was watching her, and I lay down for a minute or two, and the next time I looked for her, she was gone."

"Why did you let yourself fall asleep?"

I don't know what to say. Yes, I fell asleep, but Toby should have done what I told her.

"Ok, Robin," Bill says. "Let me tell you about my lesson in responsibility." He pauses and then says, "When your grandmother died, I wasn't at home."

He pauses again to clear his throat and make sure I'm listening. "I was leaving early to go to a church meeting in Boston. I was hoping to be elected to the Northeast Region Unitarian Council, and I felt I needed to be at that meeting to do a little politicking.

"Helen got up to make breakfast and to see me off. I knew by the way she looked that morning that she wasn't feeling well. But Helen was never one to complain. I asked her if she was OK, and she said she just had a little headache. She got migraines, and sometimes they were quite bad.

"She came to the door with me. I hugged her, and when I looked at her again, I knew something was wrong, but I really wanted to go to that meeting. I asked her if she had her migraine medication, and she said she did. I told her that I'd call her sometime in the afternoon if I got a chance and try to be home by 6:00 p.m."

Bill stopped for a minute. I could tell that he was somewhere else, thinking, I guess, about Helen and having trouble finishing the story.

"Later, I wondered if maybe she didn't tell me the truth about how she was feeling because she knew how important that meeting was to me. Anyway, I never got a chance to call home. We think that in the early afternoon Helen collapsed. A neighbor had seen her at the mailbox out on the road about noon. She yelled hello to her, but Helen didn't answer.

"Anyway, I didn't get home until almost seven. I found her lying on the living room floor. She must have been trying to call someone because the phone was off the hook and the receiver was lying by her body."

Now, Bill is choking on his words. He pauses again to clear his throat, and then he says, "She was already dead." He looks straight at me and adds, "Claire holds me responsible for her mother's death. When you guys were out here after Helen's funeral, I hadn't really been able to process what had happened. I never told Claire how bad I felt about Helen's death, so she has never really forgiven me."

Bill ends his story. He looks sad and I feel sad too. I didn't know my grandmother very well, but from what I can remember from when she and Bill visited us right before Toby was born, my grandmother was a happy person, who sat on the floor and played with me. But the situations aren't the same. They're not.

Bill looks at me, and then he smiles softly. "You need to talk to your parents. But before you do that you need to really think about what happened out on that island on Friday, really think about what you did and didn't do and about how it contributed to what happened."

I don't know what to say. I feel the fight-or-flight response kick in, but I don't do anything. I just stand there until finally I blurt out, "So you think I'm to blame for Toby's . . . disappearance."

I can't say the other D-word. I'm sure we'll find her. We have to find her. She has to be OK.

"I'm just saying you need to be honest with yourself and your parents. You need to take some responsibility."

"Responsibility? Toby didn't do what I told her to do. How can that be my responsibility?"

"After Helen died," says Bill, "Everybody said it wasn't my fault, but I couldn't help thinking that it was and that haunted me. I had to admit my responsibility to myself, before I could find some closure and move on.

"I hope we find Toby and that she's OK. But regardless of what happens, you and your parents—especially you and Claire—are going to have to look at how this happened and take some responsibility."

Responsibility. The fact is Toby didn't listen to me and something bad happened. She got too near the water, or she fell in and who knows what happened. But it wasn't my fault.

As I'm bringing my suitcase down the stairs, I hear Bill talking with someone at the door.

"Robin and Claire are flying home this afternoon, so he really can't talk."

I stop on the stairs. Whoever it is, is asking for me. My heart jumps.

I guess Bill didn't realize that I was standing on the stairs because he seems surprised when I appear out of nowhere. Now I can see whom he's talking to and I was right—it's Maude. She looks different—no torn jeans and T-shirts. She's wearing a yellowish skirt and blouse. She looks amazing!

"Hi, Robin." she says, with kind of a half smile.

I step beside Bill.

"We need to leave in about fifteen minutes," he says, and then turns around and heads back toward the kitchen.

"You're going home?" Maude asks.

"Yeah," I say. Seeing her again, I'm captivated. But I realize I owe her an explanation, now that she's here. "Mom has to go back home. There's a work emergency. And I have to go with her."

"You have to go?"

"Yeah."

The expression on her face subtly changes from a half smile to something more melancholy. "You couldn't talk them into staying for just a couple more days?"

"No, they're pretty unhappy with me, and Mom has to be home for a big work meeting tomorrow."

"Oh, that's too bad," Maude says.

For a moment, neither of us says anything. I feel all mixed up inside: happy she came by to see me, but wishing more than anything that we could have another day together.

"A friend of mine is lending me her car, and I'm planning to drive down and take the ferry over to Isle au Haut, probably on Thursday." She shifts her feet as if she's nervous, and then says, "So anyway, I thought I'd invite you to ride along. It would just be a day trip, and we'd have to leave early to catch a boat and have enough time on the island. But . . . I guess that's not possible."

I want so badly to say yes. This is what I've wanted since the day we met on the beach, and now I realize that she wants it too. But before I can even respond, I feel a cold presence behind me. It's Mom.

"Oh, hello, Mrs. Steele," says Maude.

Mom looks toward Maude and simply nods her head.

"Robin, we have to leave. Say goodbye and come join your Dad and me in the kitchen."

"I wish I could stay," I say. I don't know what else to say. But I feel really miserable, and I hope Maude realizes that.

"I understand," she says.

There's another pause. I can feel Mom behind me, and I know she'll say something else embarrassing if I don't let Maude go. "Goodbye, I really enjoyed meeting you."

"I did too, Robin."

As she's turning to go, she stops and hands me a slip of paper. It's her email address.

"Email me if you can," she says. Then she turns, and I watch her walk back toward the beach.

Part 2

Seattle

CHAPTER TEN

Back to Normal

"Look Robbie!"

I'm standing by the stunted little tree, staring out at the water, and listening to someone calling my name. The sun is shining brightly, and yet everything seems hazy. I'm sweating and my heart is pounding. It's Toby. I know it's Toby. But where is she? I look around, but she's not there. I run around and around the island, frantically yelling her name—but no Toby. And yet I keep hearing her call my name.

"Look Robbie! Wake up!"

My eyes pop open. I've had this nightmare almost every night for the first week since we returned to Seattle. I haven't said anything to Mom. We're hardly speaking, and I'm not sure how much she'd care.

Mom has been working extra hours after a staff cut at her job. She's hardly ever home. I may see her when I come down for breakfast, but she's usually on her iPhone talking with Dad in the morning. Otherwise, she's out the door and heading for work by 7:30. The other thing Mom does is spend time in Toby's room. One night I woke up about midnight and had to use the bathroom. The door to Toby's room was open a crack and I could just see Mom sitting on Toby's bed. She was folding and unfolding one of Toby's favorite shirts. It creeped me out.

Because Mom's not really at home much, Aunt Donna, her older sister, is staying with us for a while. She's doing the housework, and she and Mom go to the co-op once a week to buy groceries. But I think she is here mostly to watch me

In fact, Mom and Donna are so different that when I was a kid, I thought one of them must have been adopted or left on my grandparents' doorstep in a basket. Donna's tall like Mom, but not husky at all. In fact, she is so thin that she looks almost sickly. Both Mom and Donna are runners. But they have really different personalities. Mom can be so intense, while Donna is pretty laid back. Before Mom started working all the time, they would get together to run two or three times a week. Donna lives on the east side of Lake Washington. She has a big house in a place called Woodinville, and even though she's only in her forties, she's already retired. Dad says she made a wad of money working for a big technology company on the Eastside.

It was Donna who mentioned to Mom that she thought I should see a shrink after I told her that I wasn't sleeping very well. That's why I went to see Dr. Moore. He is a tall black man who looks like he could have been a football player. Turns out he wasn't a shrink, but rather a therapist and very soft spoken. During that first session, he kept asking me how I felt about what had happened to Toby. By the end what I felt like was screaming.

My nightmares started to fall off after the first week, but I still have problems getting to sleep. It seems like the more tired I am, the more I think about what happened on the island. And after I saw Mom sitting in Toby's room folding her clothes, I kept thinking about that too.

The truth is I'm so ready to get out of the house I can't wait for school to start. Since we got back from Maine, Mom has restricted me to helping Donna around the house, and I have a 10:00 p.m. in-bed curfew every night. Donna takes me to the public library once a week to pick up books. So I've been doing a lot of reading.

Mom says all the restrictions are because I'm in training to become a better person, one who's more responsible. My main job is to concentrate on my studies, so that I can do well in my senior year and get into college. She even wanted to take away my laptop until school started. But she had a long talk with Dad, and somehow he changed her mind. Now I'm allowed to use the laptop for school-related activities and one hour in the evening for social things. When she's home, Mom comes by my room at 10:00 p.m. sharp to make sure I'm in bed. Luckily, Donna is not so strict. When Mom's not home, she just knocks on my door and says, "Bedtime, Robin," and then goes back to her room or downstairs.

With computer privileges again, I've started emailing Mike every evening around 9:30. It makes being home seem a little less like being in a prison. When I told him what happened in Maine—my side of the story anyway—he wrote back:

Jeez Robin. What a bummer. But how can they blame you?

It felt good that he understood how I felt. Just like Mom and Donna, Mike and I are two very different animals. I'm tall and he's short. I'm kind of gangly and—well, awkward—while Mike is the best-looking Asian guy in West Lake High. He's brilliant academically, while I struggle a lot with some of my classes. When I met him, he was hanging out with a group of genius types and over-achievers at Westy, our high school. But he's not a snob, and even though the girls are all over him, he's too busy working toward his goal of getting into a good college to have a steady girlfriend.

We met in freshman Physics I. One day, I was having trouble with a problem, and he offered to help me after class. We got to talking and discovered that we both love paleontology and the idea of digging up history out of the ground. On that first day we met, I found out something else about Mike—he could be crazy funny. So as different as we are, we became best friends.

He told me about the Geology Club, and we started hanging out together regularly. We have both volunteered at the Burke Museum for the last two years. He set me up with my first date, a girl named Shelly Malone. She was another full-figured girl, but unfortunately, she caught me ogling her boobs. I think she knew what I was thinking, which effectively ended the evening. When I told Mike what had happened, we both broke up laughing. "It's happened to us all," he said.

For a minute there was a pause. Knowing Mike was waiting for me to say more, I typed:

Well, they do blame me, especially Mom. I was so fucking afraid that she was going to say I couldn't participate in choir this year. When I asked her about it right after we got back from Maine, she wouldn't say yes or no. But then she said it could be my one extracurricular activity.

As usual, Mike tried to lighten things up:

Shit, dude, that's hard! Sounds like you were lucky your parents didn't send you off to military school.

I laugh. This was so the right thing to do, Mike really knows how to crack me up. So I typed:

Well, you know how they feel about the military, particularly since Bush invaded Iraq. So there wasn't much chance I'd end up in military school. Anyway, they settled on house arrest, which is just as bad, because right now the only time I get out of the house is to go to the library with Aunt Donna.

I had gotten tired of hearing all the political talk before the trip to Maine. All Mom could talk about was how Obama was going to get us out of Iraq. Dad kept saying he hoped he'd be a "peace president." But now I wish Mom would go back to talking about politics and stop lecturing me about what happened in Maine.

As I stared at the screen, a new message popped in from Mike:

Hey dude, here's an idea. Let's accidentally meet at the library.

What a great idea! I hurriedly typed:

Mike, you're a genius! We were supposed to go today, but luckily we didn't. I'll talk Aunt Donna into going tomorrow. Where do we meet?

Mike typed back:

What time, Rob?

Two o'clock?

OK, I'll be looking at books in the teen area. Find
a way to ditch aunty and then look for me. I'll hang
out until at least 2:30 in case you're late.

Mike knows I'm usually running late. I couldn't
help smiling as I typed:

OK, dude, see you tomorrow at the library.

I just hope I can talk Donna into a library visit. She
likes it when I'm excited about reading, and we often
talk about books we've read. So tomorrow I'm going to
be real excited about picking up some new books.

*Oh no, we're never going to make it to the library on
time for me to meet Mike!* I asked Donna first thing this
morning if we could go to the library. I told her I really
wanted to pick up a couple of new books to read over
this weekend. I laid it on thick. She agreed and then
immediately began washing clothes. Washing and
drying clothes can take all day. In the summer, Mom
wants everything to be dried outside, and she never
leaves the house when anything is outside on the
clothesline.

Everything would be so much easier if I had a cell
phone. Then I could just call Mike if it looks like we're
going to be late. I had talked my parents into getting
me an iPhone like Mom's for my birthday. But that
never happened, and now it probably never will. At
least, not while I'm still living at home. This is another

reason I want to go away to college. Because once I'm living on campus, I'll have to have a phone.

Luckily, Donna is not quite as fussy as Mom. She stops for lunch at 1:00 p.m. and we are out of the house at 1:45. The library is about a mile away, and we could drive to the library in less than ten minutes. But it's a warm, sunny late-August day, and Donna wants to walk.

"Good exercise," she says.

Of course, when we get to the library, a low-rise building built between a green belt and a housing development, with solar panels on the roof, we're about fifteen minutes late. I blast through the front door and head past the central information desk toward the teen area.

"Where will you be?" I hear Donna ask from behind me.

"In Teens," I tell her as I narrowly avoid bumping into a mom shepherding her three little kids toward the circulation desk.

Teens is situated in a corner by a big window looking out at the green belt. There is a circle of cushy chairs on one side, and as soon as I walk into the circle, I see Mike talking to a girl. She is one of those cheerleader types, a blond hottie—thin with an athletic look. Mike the babe magnet is at it again.

I don't recognize the girl. Before I get close enough to say anything, Mike says something to her. She smiles and then leaves.

"Robbie Hood!" he says. "You made it."

When we first met, I wore a hoodie sometimes when we were hanging out. For some reason, Mike thought it made me look like the fictional character, so he started calling me Robbie Hood. I don't wear a hoodie much anymore, and I find the nickname a little embarrassing.

Mike keeps using it though and, I guess, because he's my best friend I haven't really tried to stop him.

"Yeah, we walked. Go figure. I should have known you'd find something to keep you occupied." I nod toward the blond who is now looking at the bulletin board right next to the big Teens area window.

"Nice girl," Mike says matter-of-factly. "She's been going to Truman. But they moved north this summer, and she'll be starting at Westy on Monday."

I sit down by Mike. "I'm so looking forward to school," I say. "Did you get your class schedule in the mail? I'm taking AP World History and AP Environmental Science. The latter, I hope, from Mrs. Daniels. Do we have any classes together?"

Mike smiles. "I've got AP Human Geography and AP Environmental Science," he says. "So we'll have, at least, AP Environmental Science together, and it should be with Mrs. Daniels."

I'm glad to hear that. I took AP Biology last spring. I had aced General Biology when I was a sophomore, but the AP class last year was tough, particularly the botany part. I worked so hard, and still only managed to get a 4. They don't give letter grades in AP classes. You're rated on a scale of 1 to 5. Anyway, I like Mrs. Daniels, but as a teacher, she's no pushover. Still, for some reason, I seem to do well in her classes.

"How come you're not taking Human Geography? Mike asks, "That class should be a snap."

"AP Biology last year was a bear. It was tougher than I thought it would be, and I only got a 4. I really need to get a 5 in another AP class, and I think Environmental Science is my best bet. And I'm taking my SATs on October eighteenth. So I'll probably take Human Geography in the spring."

"Dude, you should have taken another AP class last year," Mike says.

"Yeah, I know," I sigh. "But AP Biology was such a struggle that I'm glad I didn't."

Suddenly I realize that for the first time since I got home, I am feeling really happy. I'm not locked in the house and I'm talking with my best bro. "Anyway, I see some late-night study sessions in our academic future, Mr. Sadaka."

Mike grins. "And I thought this year would just be girls, girls, girls."

"Well, it's your choice dude," I say. "You can keep your eyes on the prize and get into Berkeley or Yale, or you can keep your eyes on the babes and end up teaching geology at some junior college and supporting a family."

"That's a tough choice," Mike says, sarcastically. "What should I do? What should I do?"

We both laugh, and then Mike asks about what happened in Maine.

"I'm really sorry to hear about your sister. Your parents must be frantic."

"You got that right, especially Mom. But I think Dad is too. He's just less emotional."

"I know that I'd be seriously upset if my little brother got lost. How are you feeling?"

"I'm so confused," I say with a shrug. "At first, I thought Toby would show up right away, like one of those bad dreams where you suddenly wake up and everything is back to normal. But she didn't and the bad dream has continued."

"So, she's just totally vanished? No clues?"

"Only her little camera, and actually I almost wish they hadn't found that."

"Why? It hasn't helped?"

"No, it hasn't helped, at least not from what we've heard. But it did give Mom another excuse to blame me for what happened."

"What?" Mike says. Of course, he doesn't understand what I'm talking about and so now I'm going to have to tell him.

"I was supposed to be watching Toby. We went out to this little island just off the shore from Bill's house. Toby went crazy after we got there, running around and taking pictures of everything like she does. They shouldn't have let her bring her camera along on the trip. Everything would have been different if she hadn't had that camera."

"Anyway, I told her and told her to stay away from the water. Then I put on my headphones and started listening to my MP3 play list. I guess I sorta got too much into the music, and the next thing I knew Toby was gone."

Mike gives an audible sigh and sits back in his chair. "So why did finding her camera make things worse? Wouldn't that just confirm that she was missing?"

Leave it to Mike to get right to the point. "Yeah, it confirmed she was missing, which only served to upset my parents even more. But somehow the state crime lab was able to salvage one picture off that little junk camera."

I pause and then say, "In the picture it looks like I'm sleeping under the little scrub tree at the center of the island."

"Wow! That's bad. How did you parents handle that?"

"I think that convinced everyone that it was my fault. Nobody listened to my explanation after that. Mom essentially said—well, implied—that I was responsible for whatever had happened to Toby."

"No way dude," Mike says.

"Yeah, so now I'm trying to get my life back to normal, or as normal as it can be with Mom hating me and Toby still missing."

"What a bummer. Your whole vacation ruined. Your little sister lost, and your parents really on your case."

"That's about the size of it." I say. But even as I say that, I realize that not everything on the Maine trip was bad. After all, I met Maude.

I start to tell Mike about her, how beautiful and free she was, but I stop myself Even though I can't get Maude off my mind, it doesn't seem right to be talking about her now.

I shift in my seat and look at the big clock over the information desk. It's almost 3:00. Then I spy Donna standing by the circulation desk and looking this way.

"Oh," I say, "my aunt is waiting for me."

I stand up and grab two books from the Teen new book display.

Mike stands and we do the brothers handshake.

"Hang in there, man. After all, maybe the worst is over," says Mike.

"Yeah, maybe." I try to sound optimistic. But I'm not. Anyway, at least I'll be back in school in three days, with other things to think about—college and choir—and maybe when things get a little more back to normal, I can even tell Mike about Maude. I've wanted to email Maude since I got home, but I want to have good things to tell her when I do. So it's not the right time yet. Not yet.

Chapter Eleven

Singing in the Rain

Wouldn't you know it? After being sunny and warm for the first week of school, it rains on the first day of choir practice. I've finally settled into my school routine. Up at 6:30, dress, eat breakfast, and catch the bus to school. Except for choir practice days, I am home and studying by 4:00, and no excuses. But after mulling it over, Mom did agree to let me help struggling students in the geology lab on Thursday afternoons. She had to admit it will look good on my college applications, and that's Mom's main interest in me now—making sure I get into college, and guess who is volunteering in the geology lab the same day—Mike.

The first day of school Mom also said I could take a hiatus from seeing Mr. Moore. I had complained that my visits to the therapist were just stressing me out and suggested that I would focus better on my studies if I could stop seeing him until I got back into a good routine at Westy. That did the trick.

"OK," Mom said. "for a few weeks anyway. We'll see how you do and then reevaluate. But remember, your focus has to be on your studies, not on socializing."

Life is about halfway back to normal. School has started. I'm seeing most of my friends at school and getting away from my home detention, Monday through Friday. But things at home haven't changed much. If anything, they've gotten worse. Mom is working long hours, and some days she already looks exhausted when I see her in the morning.

They still haven't found Toby. "No good leads," is what she usually says when I ask her what's going on in Maine. And I can tell she's getting really frustrated. Increasingly, she'll add, "They're not doing enough," or, "They've given up on finding her."

I haven't gotten to talk with Dad since the Sunday before school started. He called to talk about school, but Mom took the call and spent about twenty minutes questioning him about the police investigation. By the time she gave the phone to me, all he had time to say was, "Good luck with your classes, Robin," and "Stay focused." Oh, and that he "missed me."

For the first few weeks after she disappeared, I still thought Toby would just show up. We would get a call from Dad saying that she had just walked in off the beach and told Dad and Bill that she had been out looking for treasure, or maybe captured by pirates from whom she had just escaped—something crazy like that. But now I'm pretty sure that's not going to happen.

Anyway, it's back to choir with today's rehearsal, and that means that for a few hours I can get lost in what I like to do best: sing.

Mrs. Walker is the choir director at West High. She's in her thirties and has a music degree from University of Washington. Physically, because she's got a husky build, she reminds me a little bit of Mom, even though she's shorter and a blond.

After being in the choir with her for three years, I realize that Mrs. Walker is a master at getting us ready for any performance, no matter how hard the music, or how much we are struggling with a particular song. She's very patient, and she lets us have fun with the music. But she also expects us to work hard on every piece, and once she makes up her mind about a piece of music or a person, it is hard to get her to change.

"Don't worry," she'll say, if we're still not quite where she wants us to be in our final rehearsal. "It will all come together when we perform it."

And you know what? It mostly does.

Stepping through the doorway of the auditorium, I see a lot of people I know from last year, including Keira and Kelly; Steven, Alan, Darrick, Geoff, Marcus and Dixon Archer, all guys from the tenor section; and big George Little, a bass. But I see a lot of new faces, especially in the sopranos and altos.

Keira Sanchez waves to me as I walk down the nearest aisle. We rehearse in the main school auditorium, Elmer Johnson Hall, where we sing every Wednesday afternoon at 3:00. I wave back to let her know I've seen her. With auburn hair and a golden tan, Keira Sanchez catches people's attention wherever she goes. She's got a soft infectious smile and a great voice. I think singing comes easy for her. Her mother is a singer and teaches voice. With Sandy Clifford graduating, Keira will likely be this year's soprano lead.

"Robin!" somebody yells. It's Kelly. She's standing with some of the other altos and waving and motioning me to come over.

As I start toward Kelly, Mrs. Walker walks into the auditorium. She's wearing the womanish looking suit she always wears for rehearsals, along with a solid-colored, usually light blue or lavender, blouse. Today she's carrying a folder full of music that she sets down on a long table at the side of the room, next to the music department's old piano.

"OK, everyone, let's get up on the stage, and arrange ourselves by parts. If you're not sure which part you sing, see me after the rehearsal. But for now, just pick a group."

There is a lot of jostling as people head for one of the designated groups on the stage to get themselves arranged. But it's much easier this year because the school had the auditorium partially remodeled over the summer, and now the left half of the stage has choir steps.

Because I'm tall, I stand in the back row of the tenors. The guy in front of me in a familiar beige blazer and dark brown slacks is helping some of the new guys get settled on the steps. He is Dixon Archer, one of the two regular tenor soloists and the tenor lead for the last two years.

"Get settled, please," Mrs. Walker says. There is some frantic movement as everyone rushes to find their spot, then suddenly the rusting stops.

"For those of you who don't know me, I'm Mrs. Walker, the West High choir director. This choir performs four concerts throughout the year: one at the end of October, a holiday concert the first week of December, a spring concert in March, and an end-of-year concert in mid-May. How many of you are new this year?"

Almost a third of the choir raises their hands.

"OK, that's a lot." Then she pauses as if she's thinking. "We have six weeks to get ready for our first performance. That means we've got a lot of work to do, and everybody needs to know who his or her section lead is. Therefore, as I call the names of the four section leaders, I want them to step down in front of their sections: Keira Sanchez, soprano lead; Maggie James, alto lead; Dixon Archer, tenor lead; and George Little, bass lead."

The leads step down. Then Mrs. Walker nods, and they all walk over to the long table and start picking up music for their sections.

There's more jostling as the leads hand out copies of two songs, and some of the new people want to move around so that they can to see Mrs. Walker more clearly.

"OK, everybody," Mrs. Walker says again. "I'd like the really tall people to stand in the back of each section so that everyone can see me."

There's more jostling, but finally everybody settles down.

"How many have sung before in a church or school choir? Raise your hands."

About 90 percent of the choir raises their hands.

She glances over the choir. I guess to see who hasn't raised their hands. "OK, that's good."

"Now how many of you want to go on to sing in either a college choir, or a semi-professional or community choir?"

This time the hands drop off to about 50 percent of the choir. I'd love to sing when I go to college. But my first priority is getting into a school that has a good geology or earth science program. It would be real plus though if the school had a decent choir.

"And finally, how many of you can read music?"

Wow, a lot of the kids, especially the girls, can read music. I suddenly feel a little nervous because I really struggle sometimes with the notation. I took guitar lessons for a half a year when I was in middle school. But I felt clumsy with the guitar, had trouble practicing, and didn't much care for the teacher. I dropped out and have now forgotten most of what I learned.

"So," Mrs. Walker says, and then she takes a minute, as if she's trying to decide exactly what to say. But I remember her Opening Day lecture from last year, so I can guess what's coming.

"We have a lot of experience in this choir, but maybe not so much formal training. Anyway, one thing I want everyone to understand is that we are a semi-professional choir. I expect you to attend rehearsals, to stay focused when you're here, and to work with your fellow singers to create the kind of music, the sound and harmonies, that I believe this choir should be able to produce."

She pauses again and then adds, "Hard work and team work make a good high school choir."

"Any questions?"

One of the new members in our section starts to raise his hand, but then puts it back down when he sees that no one else has raised theirs.

"If you need to see me, I'm in my office Tuesday and Wednesday mornings at 7:30, or you can talk to me after rehearsals. But I'm leaving twenty minutes at the end of each practice for singers to meet with their section leaders, and I'd like all of you to stay and do that for at least the first couple of weeks. Another option is for those of you who are taking my music appreciation course on Tuesday and Thursday mornings to see me before or after class."

I wish I could have taken that course this fall. It might have helped me get a better understanding of notation. But Mom wouldn't let me because I need to take all the hard courses I can this semester to show a prospective college that I am serious about my studies.

I guess I can see her point. But that means I'll continue to struggle through the first few practices with each new song.

"OK singers, let's get started."

It turns out to be a pretty normal first rehearsal. Everybody is a little rusty and some even seem a little nervous. My own voice sounds scratchy, even after we do our warm-ups, which is odd, since I usually don't have any problems with my voice. Sometimes I get a little sore throat after a long practice, but it never bothers me during a performance.

All the tenors meet with Dixon when practice ends. He's a good—but not great—singer, but he can read music and he's got a big range. Dixon can easily hit a tenor C, one octave above middle C. In music notation it is called a C5. I often struggle to hit tenor C. Dad calls me a second tenor, and says most second tenors struggle to hit a tenor C. So anyway, it's important that I have a clear voice when I sing, and to make every practice. That way I get myself in a place where I have a chance to hit those high notes, like a tenor C.

I don't know why, but Dixon and I have never really hit it off. Maybe that's because he's a hardcore academic snob. He takes only the toughest classes. He's been in student government and currently serves as president of the chess club. The people he hangs out with are all high school success stories. Mike knows him, but they don't seem to be friends.

This is Dixon's second year as the tenor lead. Mike Harvey, who was the tenor lead before Dixon, encouraged me to try out to sing solos. But Dixon never has. When I asked him if he would sound out Mrs. Walker about my soloing, he said I'd have to talk to her myself. But he suggested that before going to her I should work harder on my voice and master more music notation.

While that may have been good advice, I found it really discouraging. Anyway, I didn't talk to Mrs. Walker until the choir season was almost over. And, of course, she said it was too late for me to get a solo together and that we could talk about it again in September.

One of the new guys, the one with unruly dark hair who had started to ask Mrs. Walker a question, but had then dropped his hand when he realized that nobody else had raised theirs, asks Dixon what we normally do at these short meetings after the main rehearsals.

"What's your name again?" Dixon asks.

"Phineas Alexander," the new guy says. "But everybody just calls me Phinney." A couple of the older guys grin when they hear his name.

"OK, Phinney," Dixon says, smiling as he says the new guy's name. "Basically, we talk about problems we are having with particular pieces of music, and as it gets closer to a performance, we might have a short sectional to practice our particular parts."

"Oh," says Phinney. "With or without the piano?"

"Depends on if any of the other groups are using it. If we ask Mrs. Walker, she will usually stay and accompany us. But it actually works almost as well if I sing our starting note and then we listen to each other as we sing."

The new guy kind of frowns as if he's wondering how that would really work. But Dixon's right. Listening to each other over time brings us all together as a group.

Phinney smiles, "Alright. I'll be here."

Phinney has another one of those infectious smiles. I have a feeling he's going to be fun to sing with.

We don't stay for a full twenty minutes. As we break up and everybody starts to leave, I catch up with Kelly Branson. She's laughing with a couple of other girls. But when she sees me coming her way, she raises her arms and says, "Robbie," another nickname I dislike. Then she gives me a big hug.

"Are you OK?" she asks.

"Yeah," I say, not quite sure how to respond. Has she heard about Toby's disappearance?

"I just heard about Toby. That's so awful."

I wonder what she has heard. I start to feel anxious. "Have they found her?"

"No," I say. I don't want to go into details. Telling Mike everything was one thing. But telling anybody else that my parents think I'm responsible for what happened would just give people ideas. And would make what happened in Maine a general topic of conversation.

So before she can ask me any more questions, I change the subject. "Ready for another year of singing?"

Kelly throws her head back, sending her long red hair whipping around, then smiles and says, "Definitely, our last year at Westy. Can you believe it? Are you finally going to solo?"

I sigh. "Yeah, I'm going to talk to Mrs. Walker. I really want to solo, and this year will be my last chance to do it at Westy. But I've also got to do well in my classes, or my parents will go ballistic. And I want to have a shot at getting into certain schools."

"Cool," says Kelly.

"What about you? You still planning to go to a community college?" I like Kelly. It's hard not to like Kelly, and we both really love to sing. But academics aren't her strong point.

"If I want to become a veterinary assistant, I guess I have to."

Kelly glances over to where two of her friends are obviously waiting for her. She's such a happy, positive person almost everyone likes Kelly. But she's certainly no hottie, and I've overheard one of the high school princesses refer to her as "too pudgy." I'm sure she's heard that kind of remark too. But you'd never know it if she has. The other thing about Kelly is that she can seem kinda outrageous with her flamboyant dresses, wild hair, and self-deprecating humor. But she's really a sweet person.

"Look, a few of us are planning to get together on some Saturdays to practice parts at Angela Potter's house. Not this week, but probably as we get closer to the first performance. Angela says she'll have pizza. So it will be sort of like a party, a singing party. You should think about coming. It'll be fun."

It sounds like it will be fun. But I know Mom will never let me go to anything remotely resembling a party on a Saturday or any other day during the week for that matter.

"Sure," I say without hesitation. I don't want to tell her no right away.

"Great," she says. "I've got to go. Mary, Angela and I are going to go study over at Mary's house."

But just as she turns to go, Kelly stops and says in a rather low voice, "Can we can get together sometime to have coffee? I'd like to tell you about my summer and, you know, catch up."

I don't know what to say. Do I want to have coffee with Kelly? Anyway, it's not an option. Prisoners can't go out for coffee.

There's a pause and finally Kelly says, "OK, but think about it. It's not every day you get a coffee invitation from a fabulously charming and vivacious redhead."

She gives me that big Kelly smile and then adds, "Great to see you Robbie, really great." She doesn't wait for a response. She waves her hand in the air, and before I can say anything she is gone.

It is still raining when I leave school, but I don't mind because my head is full of music. As I head for my bus, I start singing Dylan's *Forever Young*. I'm feeling good. Everything is cool. My friends are still my friends. I'm in choir again. My wishes for this year are going to come true. I'm determined to make this a great year, grade-wise and singing-wise. Things are finally getting back to normal. I can feel it.

CHAPTER TWELVE

"You've Got to be Kidding"

It's Thursday afternoon and I'm working in the geology lab. I've been hoarse again off and on all day. That's a little disturbing. Mike's here, and we're mostly helping sophomores figure out how to identify different minerals from rock samples. That's basic geology, but after almost three weeks of class, some of these kids are still so confused.

"I can't believe some of these questions," I tell Mike.

Not quite as many people showed up for lab today, but it seemed like everyone who showed up had a question.

"They're asking about things they think they'll get questions on in their first quiz," Mike says.

"Yeah, like what's granite? Anybody who has read the first couple chapters of the textbook should be able to describe granite."

Mike just smiles. "You don't remember how nervous you were those first few weeks in Physics I."

"Yeah, I remember. But this is basic geology."

"A lot of these kids aren't that interested in geology. They're just taking Geology One to fill a science requirement."

The truth is, I struggle to be a barely above average student. I'm not a Brainiac like Mike, but someone with one big goal—to become a paleontologist. And I know my geology. For my eighth birthday, my parents got me a rock and mineral guide. You know, the kind with descriptions and color pictures of rocks and minerals. After Toby was born, and everything at my house was about the new baby, that book became my best friend. I took it everywhere with me. I picked up rocks and brought them home, and I set up a samples table in my bedroom.

Mom got upset when she found out about the rocks. She thought they were a mess.

But then Dad said, "That's what scientists do, collect and study things."

She couldn't very well criticize me after that. So I dove right into learning about the different kinds of rocks, and then into the broader concepts of geology, and finally how geological strata reveal the story of Earth's history.

"When are you going to do your early action applications?" Mike asks.

"I don't know, but Dad has to get back here soon because his classes start soon. Then we'll sit down and rough out the applications for the UW and Western."

"What about Berkeley?"

"Yeah, I want to apply to Berkeley, but I know I'll have to wait to do that until after I get my first semester grades in February. If I can ace my regular courses, I think I can push my GPA up over three point. I need a four point if I want a shot at getting into Berkeley. What about you?" I ask.

"I started working on my applications last weekend. But I'm a little nervous."

"Dude, you nervous?"

"Yeah, I am. There's no assurance I'll get into either Yale or Berkeley."

"You're practically a straight-A student!"

"Yeah, but thanks to American Literature my sophomore year—you know the year I took that AP Chemistry class that I thought would be so easy and then had to work my butt off to get an A. Anyway, thanks to Mr. Shelley and American Literature, I've only got a 3.87 GPA."

"Well, don't forget Kati Monroe."

Mike shrugs uncomfortably. Is he blushing? I can't really tell. "Yeah, Kati," he says, almost wistfully.

The only girl I've ever known Mike to go overboard for was Kati our sophomore year. She was tall—as tall as me—blond and very athletic. She was also smart. She sat next to Mike in American Literature, and you could tell she was always on his mind. He would move around in his seat and steal a glance at her and not concentrate on class, which was really out of character for Mike. As far as I know, they never even spoke. But somewhere along the line Mr. Shelley saw what was going on and moved Mike to the front of the class.

"So it will be easier for you to concentrate," is what he told Mike. But Mike's mind was still on Kati all that semester.

"Yeah, Kati was hot," Mike, says again with a sigh.

"Lucky for you she moved out of state for her junior year," I say with a sly grin.

Mike shrugs. "Yeah, lucky." He sighs.

While kidding Mike about Kati is fun, I decide it's time to change the subject. I know how it is to be embarrassed about something and not want to talk about it.

"So you got a B in American Literature. So what! Do you think the colleges will even care that you got a B in a literature course?"

"I think Yale and Berkeley will care about all my grades, particularly since I'm applying to do undergraduate work."

"But we're science guys, and what does literature have to do with science?"

"Yeah, I know what you mean. I can't really get into reading fiction. Science fiction is OK, but definitely not that fantasy stuff or those old classics that the teachers like so much," Mike adds. "I read science, academic and popular."

"Yeah," I say. "Talking about metaphors and symbolism in class is just plain boring. I remember reading *Frankenstein* in Mr. Shelley's sophomore Literature class. I couldn't put it down. It was so creepy and the main character, Victor goes crazy. But when we had to analyze it in class. It just killed my interest in the book."

"That's right, dude. I'm not interested in literature," Mike says, doing a very funny imitation of those dweeby announcers on public television.

We both laugh.

"Give me a book by Timothy Ferris, or Brian Greene, or Stephen Jay Gould. Those are the guys I want to read."

"Yeah," I say, "Stephen Jay Gould called himself a 'dinosaur nut.'"[1]

Two months after Toby was born, Dad gave me a paperback copy of *Dinosaur in a Haystack*. As it turned out, the author of this mysterious and wonderful book of essays was a paleontologist, Stephen Jay Gould. In this book he wrote about all kinds of stuff. Things like how much he loved the dinosaur exhibits at the American Museum of Natural History. He grabbed me right away with that story and the one about how volunteers from Milwaukee Public Museum, searching for dinosaur bones in North Dakota, found evidence to substantiate the theory that a catastrophic event caused the dinosaur extinction 65 million years ago. Gould is my favorite science writer.

I wanted to write my literature class paper on *The Conchologist's First Book*, a controversial book on shells attributed to Edgar Allen Poe, America's first great writer of horror fiction. Gould told the history of *The Conchologist's First Book* in *Dinosaur in a Haystack*, and why he thought the book was important, even though most people at the time said it was just a hack job. For one thing, it was mostly plagiarized, which I thought would make it even more interesting. But when I got my class paper proposal back from Mr. Shelley, all he had written on it was, "You've got to be kidding!"

In *Dinosaur in a Haystack*, Gould writes about science and natural history. I can't say I completely understood all his essays at first. Some I had to read two or three or more times before I could figure out what he was saying. But Gould loved science so much that it was exciting just to read what he had to say. His essay on the K-T Extinction got me really thinking for the first time about how science is supposed to operate. Gould made thinking about natural history so much fun that after reading his book, I was hooked. I knew I had to become a paleontologist.

"So why are you waiting for your Dad to come home to start your early action applications?" Mike asks.

"I'll need a little help filling out those applications, and Dad's the logical choice to do that."

"Can't you ask your mom for help?"

"You've got to be kidding. She's hardly ever home and when she is, she treats me like I'm a criminal on probation."

"That's too bad. No word yet on Toby?" Mike asks.

"No," I say with a shrug.

After an uncomfortable moment when neither one of us seems to know what to say. Mike asks, "So she's been missing for almost a month. Isn't it likely she drowned?"

It's like someone hit me in the stomach. I feel woozy, like maybe I'm going to be sick. "I can't think about that. If I do, I get really anxious, and I can't get my mind back on school or anything else."

"Doesn't your mom realize how important this year is for you?"

As September has moved along, Mom has becoming more and more distant. Some days I don't see her at all, which is actually just fine because when I do, I can tell what she's thinking. And sometimes it seems like she can hardly stand looking at me.

"Oh, she keeps saying that studying has to be my top priority. But when it comes to helping me, I'm not sure I'd want her to try. She's not very patient, especially now. And she's even started acting crazy about little things, like me not wanting to help Donna with the dishes when I want to actually use my one hour of 'personal' computer time on the computer."

"You know your applications need to be in by November fifteenth."

"Yeah, I'm taking my SATs October eighteenth. Dad will be here this weekend, I hope, and we'll get the applications drafted. Then when I get my SAT scores, I'll add them and mail everything out."

"That's cutting it pretty close. Are you nervous about taking the SATs?" Mike asks.

"I'm nervous about everything—my SATs, my GPA, my AP class grades. I've got a 2.95 GPA. That's what Dad calls a 'gentleman's B.' But I have to keep working hard this year and increase my GPA to at least a solid three, ace Advanced Geology and my other regular classes, and score fives, or at least fours, in AP Environmental Science and AP World History."

"So when do you want to get together to work on AP stuff?"

"Well, I've got to clear that with Mom."

"What? I thought she wanted you to concentrate on your homework"

"Yeah, but this prisoner has to clear all his visits with friends with the prison warden, even when it's to do homework."

"Boy, that is hard, dude."

"Can you come over to our house?"

Mike frowns but doesn't say anything. As much as we are friends, I know he doesn't like to get mixed up in family disputes. In his house, nobody gets mad or says bad things to anyone else. It sounds unnatural to me.

"Mom's not likely to be there, and Donna's OK. She won't bother us."

"Sure," Mike says. "Maybe after your mom sees that we are really studying, she'll let you have a furlough to come over to my place."

I doubt that's going to happen, but I don't say that to Mike.

"I'll ask Donna to talk with Mom. If I talk with her, she'll probably just accuse me of asking for more privileges so I can go out and goof off. But maybe Donna can convince her." Mike's right. I can't let myself get trapped in Mom's negativism, and constantly thinking about what happened in Maine is just that kind of trap. I've got to stay focused on school.

The class I'm most looking forward is Advanced Geology. There is not a separate AP Geology course, but a few high schools have an advanced class, mainly for seniors who love the subject, and luckily, Westy is one of those schools. Everyone says that we have the class because Mrs. Daniels lobbied so hard to teach it.

So I'll have Mrs. Daniels for two classes, AP Environmental Science and Advanced Geology. I'm confident I'll do well in both. Then I'm taking AP World History—another class that should be easy—along with Algebra II and Spanish II Conversation. I can visualize getting 3 A's, a couple of 5's in the AP classes, and hopefully a "gentlemen's B" in Spanish II. I struggle with languages. I won't even get into what happened when I tried to take German my sophomore year. What a disaster! But Spanish isn't German.

Mike and I go over some of our AP notes before we leave the lab, so I don't get home until almost 6:00. When I walk into the house, I hear Mom's voice. She stomps into the dining room as I'm dropping my books on the table and demands to know why I'm home so late.

"Robin, you need to be home by five on Thursday, every Thursday. You can't be spending three hours at that lab. I know you're goofing off with your friends, and you don't have time to do that."

"Mike and I were staying at the lab to work on homework," I say. But Mom is undeterred.

"I don't want to hear any excuses."

Donna is standing at the entrance to the kitchen watching Mom's slow burn.

"Mike can come by on Thursdays after lab, and you two can work here for an hour or so before dinner. But I want you to be home by five, period. And if you can't do that, you'll have to quit volunteering at the lab."

My heart is pounding. I don't know what to say. She's got to be kidding. But I know she's not. I'm a prisoner on work release each day to attend school, but I have to be back inside the jail by a certain time or else.

I go up to my room and find Moon Pie lying on my bed. She looks up at me when I come into the room. But I'm so nervous that I just pace around my room. Finally, I sit down on the bed, and Moon Pie lets me scratch under her neck. She's warm, and it's nice to hear her purr. Slowly my heart stops pounding.

After a minute, I reach over and grab my tattered copy of *Dinosaur in the Haystack* from the bookshelf. Regardless of how much Mom shouts, I have to stay calm and focused. Rereading one of Gould's essays will help me get my mind off Mom's vendetta. I pick the one about how Hollywood got it all wrong when they made the book *Frankenstein* into a movie. Gould's idea in that essay, about something important being badly misunderstood, really connects with me right now. That's what has happened with Toby's disappearance. I'm being blamed, but it wasn't really my fault.

And reading Gould always brings me back to the reason I'm working so hard to get into college. I want more than anything to be a paleontologist. Later, when I can't sleep, I go downstairs to get some milk from the refrigerator. I'm surprised to see Donna is sitting at the kitchen table looking at an old newspaper. She looks up when I come in.

"Can't sleep?" she asks.

"No."

"Me neither."

I take a carton of milk out of the refrigerator and pour it into a glass.

"She's under a lot of stress," Donna says as I'm putting the milk away.

"Yeah," I say, as if I don't really care—because I guess I don't.

"She's under a lot of pressure, and it's not just worrying about Toby, but also about her job."

I look at Donna. What's she talking about? But I'm too tired to ask, and I'm determined not to get caught up in Mom's craziness.

"She'll come around," Donna says. "Just give her time."

She's got to be kidding. Even if they find Toby alive, I'm afraid she may never get off my case. That thought almost takes my breath away. *If they find Toby alive.*

"Well, I'm going to bed." As Donna stands up, she hands me a folded piece of paper. It's a note from Mom. As she walks out of the kitchen, I open the note and read:

Robin, your dad will be flying home on Saturday.

CHAPTER THIRTEEN

Hope

A big, bright, blue and red poster of Obama with the word HOPE in big letters under his image greets everyone coming in our front door. You can't walk into our house without knowing where this family stands politically. If there are blue states, this is certainly a blue house, at least when it comes to Barack Obama.

Mom was so proud of that poster when she brought it home about a month after she started working part-time for the Obama campaign last winter. She said the poster showed that we were part of something big. Obama was going to bring the country together and get us out of Bush's war in Iraq, and that was really important. Both Mom and Dad went to their caucus in March as Obama delegates. And after Obama won the Washington caucus, Mom could hardly talk about any-thing else.

That seems like it was a long time ago now. I've never had much interest in politics. And I didn't really like the poster when Mom brought it home. I thought it made Obama look kind of weird. But now the HOPE poster is one of the few things that I look forward to seeing when I come home. Mom was happier then—after being pretty grumpy when she had to return to work full-time. For about seven months after the first of the year, she was almost back to the mom I remember before Dad left the University.

Since Mom's note announcing that Dad is coming home, whenever I look at the Obama poster with the big red HOPE on it, I immediately think about how much I'm hoping that Dad's return will finally change things for the better.

"That's great, dude," Mike says, when I tell him at lunch that Dad will be home tomorrow. "Now you'll be able to get started on your early admission applications."

"Yeah, I hope so, and maybe he can talk Mom into cutting me some slack on all her rules."

"Yeah," Mike says.

"Except, how is it going to work having two parents at home? Dad might be a tougher prison guard than Aunt Donna, and I'll go crazy if I have two parents ragging on me all the time about what happened with Toby."

"Any news on the Toby front?"

"I haven't heard any. But maybe Dad will have some when he gets home. Mom doesn't tell me anything."

"So what do you think happened to her, Robbie?"

"I don't know. I don't know what to think," I say hesitantly, though that's not really what I'm thinking. What I really think—and I'm admitting this for the first time—is that Toby is probably dead.

"Do you miss her?"

What a crazy question. Miss Toby? She is such a pain, an eight-year-old drama queen who always has to be the center of attention. But even as I think about her and how irritating she is . . . was, I realize that something inside me hurts. I don't want her to be dead. I want her to come back, maybe with a different personality. But I want her to be alive. And if she is dead . . . well, I don't want to think about that.

Luckily, the bell rings before I have to answer Mike. I shrug. It's a "yes" shrug, but he may or may not realize that; then we head in different directions to our separate classes.

I'm on my way to AP World History in the mass confusion between second and third lunches when I hear someone call my name. It's Kelly.

She's wearing one of those flowery dresses—she calls them her peasant dresses—that she likes so much. The school frowns on students wearing unconventional clothing. But when she got called into the office to explain why she was violating Westy's dress code, she explained that they were the only things she really felt comfortable wearing, that she made them herself, and that they did cover her whole body, unlike some of the stuff other girls in school wore. Then she gave the vice principal one of her big Kelly smiles, all warm and genuine, and I think he must not have known what to say, because he dismissed her, and the school never brought up the subject again.

We make our way through the river of students toward each other.

"Going to class?" she yells, trying to be heard over the din in the hallway.

"To AP World History and I don't want to be late."

She gives me that "can't we talk for just a minute" look. She isn't taking any AP classes, so she doesn't really understand how much pressure, how important it is to not to be late even once for an AP class. I slow down. I want to be friendly, but I can't stop.

"I can see you're in a rush," Kelly says. "It's just that some of us are going to get together a week from Saturday at Angela Potter's to practice our songs. You know, after the choir's second rehearsal."

Her voice gets a little hesitant and then she adds, "I wanted to make sure you knew about it."

"It might be tough for me to come. Mom is being pretty strict with me after . . . you know, after what happened in Maine."

She looks a little confused. Maybe she hasn't heard. But that can't be true. At least ten kids and three teachers have told me how sorry they were to hear about Toby's disappearance.

But now the crowd is thinning out, and I know I've got to get to class.

"Thanks for letting me know. But I've got to go."

"It's going to be a party, too, Angela says she's getting pizza."

"I'm not sure that will be a selling point with Mom."

Her smile kind of fades, but then she adds, "Anyway I hope you'll come."

She's really pushing this hard. I start to say I know I can't come, but then realize that I would really like to go. I haven't just hung out with a bunch of my peers since early in the summer, and having an additional group practice would be a bonus.

"OK," I say finally. "But I've got to get to class."

Before she can say anything else, I turn and head toward class. I walk into AP History just as the final fourth period bell rings.

Mom won't let me go to the airport on Saturday to pick up Dad. I try to argue with her, but she says no—no explanation, just no. Donna and I stay at home to get things ready so we can have an early dinner when they get back from the airport. I guess Dad isn't getting anything to eat on the plane.

Donna roasts a chicken and bakes some potatoes. I stir-fry some vegetables and set the table. It's hard to believe now, but it was Mom who taught me to cook—just easy stuff at first like spaghetti, eggs, and stir-fried vegetables. I ruined a lot a chard before I got that right. But I can still remember her showing me how to prepare the food, season it, and cook multiple dishes. It was the most patient I think I've ever seen her. Now it seems like she is a different person.

Mom and Dad don't get home until almost 5:00 p.m. Mom says the traffic was backed up for two miles coming back into the city. Then Dad mentions that they sat and talked for a while before they left the airport. I wonder what they were talking about?

Donna has to reheat the vegetables before we can eat, but she brings out a bottle of wine, and both Mom and Dad have a glass. Of course, I only get milk or water or juice. While we are waiting for the food Dad asks me how things are going with school.

"Fine," I say.

Mom looks like she's going to disagree. But before I can defend my statement that things are going fine at school, as opposed to, say, at home, she gets up and goes into the kitchen to help Donna.

"How are those AP classes?" Dad asks.

"OK," I say. But then I add, "They're really a lot of work, especially Environmental Science. And it's make-or-break in those AP classes because everything hinges on how you do on the final tests. I'm lucky Mike is taking that class. I just hope we can get more time to study together."

I notice Mom watching us from the kitchen. Then Dad says, "We'll talk about that later. What about your other classes?"

"I should be able to ace Advanced Geology and Algebra II, and I'm hoping I can get a gentlemen's B in Spanish Conversation II."

Dad smiles. "Sounds good. You've really come a long way with your language skills since German."

"Spanish is a lot easier than German."

We both smile.

"How's choir?"

"Great. I'm really looking forward to singing this year."

"I know you are," Dad says. "I'm glad we could let you continue in the choir."

I hear noise from the kitchen. Mom and Donna will be bringing in the food soon.

"I was really scared Mom wasn't going to let me sing," I say softly.

Dad nods. "It was something we had to talk over. But it's important you have some extracurricular activities, and I think you would have been a very un-happy camper if you couldn't sing in the choir."

"Well, yeah," I say, maybe a little too loudly.

Mom brings in the chicken on a big platter. "Having a good talk?" she asks.

"Just catching up on Robin's first few weeks in school," Dad says. "I was just telling him that three years of high school choir would look great on his col-lege applications."

Mom frowns, and then turns and goes back into the kitchen. I start to ask Dad about helping me with the early admissions applications.

"Dinner is served," Donna announces, as she and Mom bring in the rest of the food, and I decide to wait until I have another chance to talk to Dad alone.

There is a kind of pause as everyone starts eating.

Then Mom says, "Your dad and I have been talking and we've decided that I'll fly back to Maine next week."

It seems like all the air goes out of the room, and yet this is really what I've been hoping for. Let Mom go back to Maine and leave Dad and me here so that I can really get back to having a life. It's awful to say, but that's the way I feel. Anyway, I don't say anything. I just look at Mom and then back at my food. Then I notice that Donna has stopped eating too and seems to be thinking about what Mom just said. I wonder if this is the first she's heard about this plan.

"I was hoping I could go back to the Eastside now that you're back," she says.

"Could you just stay for another week Donna," Mom asks?

Donna doesn't respond.

"Why don't you go home for a couple of days and then come back on Friday," Dad says.

"How about Wednesday night?" Mom says immediately. "Jim starts teaching on Wednesday, and I'll be flying out early on Thursday morning. And we can't leave Robin here alone."

I start to say something and then stop.

"So you'll be back in a week?" Donna asks.

"Eight days at the most."

"And you've cleared this with your boss?"

The expression on Mom's face changes. She's getting irritated with Donna's questions.

"I talked with Dan. He's OK with me being gone until a week from Wednesday. We're having a bunch of closings that next weekend, and Dan will be going out of town himself on that Sunday."

Donna doesn't seem satisfied "Is there some reason that you want to go back right now? Has something else happened?"

"I don't think the authorities are doing enough to find Toby. They haven't uncovered any new leads in almost a month." Mom's voice is starting to get louder.

"They did follow up on tip about the boat that had been in the area," Dad interjects.

"But did they really?" Mom asks. "I can't believe that the people on that boat didn't see anything. The authorities should have grilled them. They just haven't spent enough time and resources on their search."

There's another long pause while we all catch our breath and work on our dinners.

"Can't Bill keep you up to date on developments until something important happens?" Donna asks finally.

Mom stares at her and sighs. "He's trying to be helpful. But you know I can't trust him to keep on top of things, to keep on pushing."

"After all this time, you're still angry with him, aren't you?"

Mom flinches. "He can't really be trusted to be there when you need him. You know that."

Donna frowns and we all go back to eating. The dinner ends quietly. It was a great meal, but my mind has drifted away and now I'm thinking about Maine.

Later that evening, after Donna leaves, I hear Mom and Dad talking quietly in the kitchen. I guess they don't see me standing just outside the doorway.

"You've got to promise me you'll come back home after you've found out whatever it is you need to find out from the authorities," Dad says.

"I need to do everything I can to find Toby. I think the authorities have given up hope because they believe she was swept out to sea by some freak wave. But how likely is that, really?"

She pauses and then adds, "I owe that to our daughter. You should understand that, Jim. I have to be sure that every possible lead or clue has been followed up on. I have to."

"I know you think you have to go, Claire," Dad says. "But you need to come back after a week unless something fundamental changes. And when you come back, we need to start getting our life back to normal."

"Getting our life back to normal!" Mom says. "How can we ever get our life back when we have lost our daughter?"

Dad sighs, and then he adds. "Don't forget you've got a job to come back to, and a son to take care of. And when you get back, we need to have an honest talk with Robin. You two need to start rebuilding your relationship."

Mom scowls. "You know he still doesn't get it. He's so immature. In his own way, Robin's just like Dad, lots of big ideas and ambitions, but you can't count on him when it's important."

It's quiet for a minute and then Mom adds, "Maybe it's in the genes."

Whose genes is she referring to, I wonder.

"That's not fair, Claire," Dad says. "He worked really hard last year in school, and it sounds like he's continuing to work hard again this year, despite all the tension and anxiety that's taken over our lives."

Just then Dad notices me watching them from the dining room. I'm glad Dad at least knows how hard I've been working. But now that I've been noticed, I decide it's time to head up to my room.

From the top of the stairs I hear Mom say, "You know he quit seeing the therapist. We can't let him screw up his own life like he has ours."

That's not fair! Dad's right. We can't get our lives back with Mom here. I just wish she'd go tomorrow. With her gone, we should at least have time to work on my early admission applications to UW and Western, and I'll have time to talk with Dad and maybe even get him to OK my going to the choir party on Saturday. I really want to go, and with Mom gone, maybe I can make that happen.

CHAPTER FOURTEEN

Maine Calling

On Sunday Bill calls from Maine. He talks to Mom first, who tells him she's flying back to Maine on Friday. I can hear Mom's side of the conversation, and it sounds like he's asking her questions. But I stop paying attention, and take the opportunity to ask Dad about getting together to start work on two early admission applications.

"Yeah, I was thinking about that on the flight from Maine," Dad says. "How about Tuesday night?"

But before we can get anything settled, Mom calls Dad to the telephone, and then comes into the kitchen. "Whose turn is it to do the dishes, Robin?"

I look at the sink. Whoops. It's filled with breakfast dishes. *How did all those get there? Oh, well.* I get up and walk over to the sink. At least, washing dishes isn't as awful as cleaning the bathroom. In general, I hate housework. You can tell that by the clutter in my room. I'm just getting into my wash and rinse routine, when Dad brings in Mom's iPhone and hands it to me.

"Bill wants to say hi."

"Hi Robin. How are things going?"

I always notice how deep his voice is when we talk on the phone. "Getting better now that Dad is home,"

I say. Then I remember that I'm in the kitchen, and that Mom is standing there listening to everything I'm saying.

"Wait a minute," I say, and I walk into the living room and sit down in a chair by a window. "OK."

"How's school?" Bill asks immediately.

"OK, so far. I like most of my classes. But since I'm a senior they are basically classes I want to take with teachers I like. And I'm back in choir." I pause and then I add, "I'm so glad they let me go back. I was afraid Mom was going to say I couldn't sing."

"I'm glad, too," Bill responds. "Are you finally going to solo?"

"I hope so. I'm waiting for Mrs. Walker to announce the date of solo rehearsals."

"What's your toughest class?"

"AP Environmental Sciences will be a challenge. I like the teacher though, and I think I can get a five if I work hard enough."

"It wasn't tough to get back to classes and studying after what happened?"

I knew what Bill was getting at, but I didn't really want to talk about the incident.

"Nah, I was actually looking forward to getting back to classes and seeing my friends."

"That's good. Sounds like it was good that you had a couple of weeks to prepare before school started."

"Man, those first couple weeks really sucked."

"How are you and your Mom getting along? Has Claire been pretty strict?"

"Strict? I feel like I'm in prison!"

Bill gives an audible sigh. "Are you still seeing the therapist?"

How did he know I was seeing Mr. Moore? Either Mom or Dad must have told him.

"Nah," I say. "It wasn't helping."

"That's too bad," he says. Then he adds, "I suggested to your mom—and I'm suggesting to you—that you two sit down and have a really honest talk. You need to open up and share your feelings."

Of course, that is the last thing I want to do, share my feelings with Mom. But I don't say anything, hoping he'll drop the subject, but I can tell after a moment that he wants to finish saying what he has to say.

"I think both of you have gotten a little off target. Sometimes grief can do that to folks."

Am I grieving for Toby? I don't think so. I'm a little sad sometimes. But I think I'm still mostly angry with her for wandering off and getting everybody so upset.

There's another pause like Bill is waiting for me to agree with him, or at least to say something. "You know, you two are a lot alike."

"That's not true," I protest. Does he really think Mom and I are alike?

"Anyway, Robin, I want you to really think about talking with your Mom. Maybe you need to initiate the conversation. Maybe she can't. Will you do that for me?"

No way. But I can't say that, so I just say, "Maybe."

I'm afraid Bill's going to ask me more questions about Mom. But he doesn't. All he says is, "OK, that's fair. You think about it."

Now I see my chance to change the subject. "I'm hoping now that Dad's home, we can work on early admission applications for the UW and Western."

"Yes, this is a big year for you, isn't it? You've got to start applying to colleges."

"Yeah, I've really got to stay focused, and I don't need the extra pressure this Toby thing has added."

"I understand," Bill says. "I'm glad your Dad is home to help you."

I wonder if Bill really does understand.

"Oh, and one last thing, Robin. I saw Maude McAndrews, and she asked me if you had a cell phone, and what the number was. I said I'd ask you."

Maude wants to call me and, of course, I don't have a phone. Everybody I know has a cell phone, but not me. I'm getting angry again. And what's even worse, she gave me her email address and now I've lost it. I was going to email her right after our first choir practice, but when I looked for the slip of paper with her email address on it, I couldn't find it. She's probably been wondering why I haven't tried to contact her. I'm such a loser when it comes to girls.

"No, prisoners aren't allowed to have cell phones. Not in this prison anyway. I thought I would get one for my birthday. But that didn't happen, and now I doubt it will happen until I get to college. I'll be sort of on work release then, and my parents will want to be able to check up on me, so they'll have to get me a cell."

Bill sighs again. I can tell he's a little unhappy with my response. "That's too bad," he says finally. "I'm sorry to hear you're so angry about what's happened. Right now, your parents are going through a lot, and they need you to work with them."

So angry! This beautiful, creative girl I met in Maine— the only good thing that happened to me on what was supposed to be my summer vacation—wants to call me and I can't give her my number. Because, unlike every other guy she knows, I don't have a phone. How am I supposed to feel about that?

After a moment of frantic thought, I do the only other thing I can think of. I give Bill my email address, and I ask him to give it to Maude.

"Sure," Bill says. "Happy to do it."

"Thanks," I say.

The next week seems to drag on and on while I wait for Mom to fly back to Maine. After talking with Bill, I keep thinking about what he said—the idea that Mom and I should have an "honest talk" about Toby. As hard as I try, I can't get that idea to go away.

The other thing that is constantly on my mind is Maude. I hadn't thought about her much since I'd gotten home. In many ways, our walks on the beach seemed like wonderful dreams, an escape from everything else that was going on those last few days in Maine.

But if she asked Bill for my cell phone number, she must be real, and she's thinking about me! Probably she just wants to remains friends. Maybe she wants more than that. A guy can dream, can't he? Anyway, I'll start checking my email every day, in case she sends me a message.

In the meantime, at choir rehearsal on Wednesday, Mrs. Walker announces that there will be short auditions for soloists right after the main rehearsal next Wednesday. "Potential soloists need to pick a piece of music and be prepared to sing it for me next week."

I look through some of the songbooks Mrs. Walker has brought for those who'll be auditioning. They're mostly show tunes and popular songs, along with some classical stuff. Of course, once you've found a couple of songs you think are possibilities, you can always find a You Tube video of someone singing that song to see how it sounds and whether it is in a good range for you.

"You going to try out?" someone asks. It's the new tenor, Phinney Kelly.

He's also looking through the songbooks. I guess he's planning to audition. I know that Dixon's going to audition, and with Phinney and me that will make at least three tenors. It looks like there will be at least three basses, maybe more, also trying out, which means that there will be six or seven guys auditioning for maybe four male soloist slots. If I want to have a shot at landing one, I better find a song that makes the most of my voice.

"Yeah," I say, "this year's my last chance."

"You're a senior, right?" Phinney asks. "You should be a shoo-in."

I don't feel like a shoo-in. Soloing is all about who sings best at the auditions. If you have a cold, or don't prepare enough, or just pick the wrong song, you probably won't get picked.

There's a lot to think about when choosing a song for an audition. It can't be too hard or too easy and it should let you to show off your voice a bit. I make myself a list of possible songs to take home with me, and Mrs. Walker also allows each of us to take home one songbook for practice. I think I'm most likely to pick a show tune, so I take something called *The Great Book of American Show Tunes from Gershwin to Sondheim*.

The other thing I'm worried about is my voice. It's been really scratchy lately. You probably wouldn't notice it when I'm singing with the other tenors. But *I* notice it—especially when I sing alone at home, which I do a lot. At home, it seems hard for me to extend my range without sounding almost hoarse. This is where I really need to talk to Dad. We'll have a lot to talk about when Mom is gone.

When I get back from rehearsal, I head for my room to look through the songbook. I'm lying on the bed and looking through the book when I hear someone coming up the stairs. It's Mom. I can tell by her footsteps. She's walks like a runner, light on her feet just like her sister. She stops at the door and, after a moment, knocks. "Robin, I need to talk with you."

I wonder if she is going to ground me again for getting home five minutes late from choir practice. Worse, I'm afraid she'll ask me about soloing. I drop the songbook on the floor on the side of my bed away from the door, grab my Advanced Geology textbook, and sit up on the bed.

"I'm studying."

"This will only take a minute."

Sure it will. I reluctantly get up and open the door. Mom looks a little less tired than usual. Maybe having Dad back home has been good for her too. She steps into the room, and I sit back down on the bed. I can tell she's a little nervous.

"So," she says, and then stops as if she's trying to decide exactly what to say. "I'm going to be really busy tomorrow. I may work late, and then your dad will be taking me to the airport early, so I can take a 7:30 a.m. flight to Boston."

There is another pause.

"Anyway, I'm hoping we can have a nice dinner tonight. Your Dad is going to get some Thai takeout from that little place down by Green Lake. I know you like Thai."

I do like Thai. But I get the feeling that telling me about dinner isn't why she came up to see me.

"I'll be gone about a week—or maybe longer. I want to stay until we find Toby. But I can't be gone any longer or I might lose my job."

"So, when I get back home, I hope I'll have some positive news about Toby. We really need to have some positive news." She pauses again and adds, "When I get back maybe you and I need to have a talk. You know, about how we feel about what happened in Maine." Mom shifts on her feet like she's a little nervous saying this.

I'm surprised, but I get the picture. Bill suggested this when we talked on the telephone, and he probably said something about it to Mom, and now she brings it up to me as though it was her idea.

"I know you think I've been too strict with you, but I had to be after what happened in Maine."

I tense up, grit my teeth, and rub my kneecaps. Too strict—she could have ruined my senior year. I want to tell her this, but I have to hold back. For now, I'll just keep my mouth shut.

She's looking at me, with a mixture of sadness and pain on her face. "So talk to your Dad if you need to while I'm gone. Donna is coming back over next week to be there the days when your dad is teaching."

What? "Why does Donna have to be here again? I can take care of myself during the day."

"Someone needs to see that things get done around the house and be around to help you stay focused."

I scowl. I can't help it. Even though the warden is leaving for a week, Donna will be around to take her place.

The expression on Mom's face changes, and she says, "OK, I know you don't like this. But a little discipline has worked. You're keeping up with your classes, and I haven't had to worry about you doing something irresponsible."

I start to object, but Mom just keeps talking. "Let's keep things the way they are for now, and you and I can talk more when I get back. OK?"

It's not really a question. It's what she's decided, and I'm supposed to just go along. So I'm not going to answer. I'm not going to say anything because it's *not* OK. But I suddenly feel I have to say something because I'm wondering why she's going on this stupid trip.

So I blurt that out, "Isn't it obvious what happened to Toby?" As soon as I say it, I know it is a mistake.

Mom's body stiffens.

"Robin, we don't know anything for sure. Toby may be lost, somewhere alone and afraid. She may not even know who she is. The only thing we really know for sure is that the authorities in Maine are either incompetent, or they just don't care. To them it's just another disappearance."

She takes a breath. She's agitated now, I can tell.

"Toby's lost, Robin. The sheriff and the state police are useless. They don't love her like we do. Sometimes, I think I'm the only one who can find her. Maybe, I'm the only one who cares enough. Anyway, it's my responsibility now."

What an outburst. She stops, and I know she's waiting for me to tell her I understand. But I don't.

"OK," I say finally, but just to get her out of my room.

It works. She turns and leaves.

Mom and Dad leave for the airport before I get up on Friday. All day at school I keep thinking about how I need to talk to Dad when I get home. He doesn't work on Fridays. "The perks of the job," he says.

Mike is waiting for me after my last class. He wants to talk. "I've got something I want to tell you," he says.

But I'm anxious to get home. "I need to get home to talk with Dad, about the choir practice tomorrow. Email me and we can talk tonight."

When I get home, Dad is there working on the computer.

"Want to work on those early admission applications this weekend?" Dad asks before I can even bring the subject up.

Already, with Mom gone, things are changing.

"Yes," I say.

We decide we'll spend Sunday afternoon on the applications. Then, while I'm feeling lucky, I bring up my solo audition and the singing party. I have a strategy for bringing up these two things together that might just work.

"I'm going to audition to solo this year. The auditions will be Wednesday after the regular rehearsal, so I'll probably be about an hour late getting home."

Dad smiles. "That's great. I know you wanted to solo last year, but it didn't work out. And thanks for letting me know. This way, I can tell Donna so she won't be worried when you're late. I think your mom told you Donna would be staying here Monday through Thursday next week."

"Yeah, she did." I try to keep from sounding too unhappy.

"Did you and she have a chance to talk some about how you both are feeling about Toby's disappearance?"

"Not really. She said something about us talking more when she gets back." I pause, knowing that anything else I say Dad will probably consider negative. But after a moment, I add, "With her attitude, I'm not sure talking will be such a good thing."

Dad frowns. "That's too bad. I don't know exactly how things have been between you two while I've been in Maine. I figure you're still both pretty stressed about Toby's disappearance, but you still need to talk."

"Yeah," I say, not very convincingly. "Do you think it's going to help her going back to Maine?"

"I don't know," Dad says. "I hope so. Anyway, she feels like she has to go."

Something has been nagging at me ever since I talked with Mike a week ago. What will happen if we never find Toby? Part of me wants to ask Dad. But part of me doesn't, and that part wins. Right now, I need to get his permission to go to the Saturday rehearsal.

"So the choir is having a Saturday afternoon rehearsal at Angela Potter's house, and it's pretty important I attend."

Dad frowns, and I know he's thinking that this request is out of the blue, and that he needs to know a lot more before he says yes.

"Tell me more," he says.

"We really need to have an extra practice before our fall performance, and it would be helpful for me in deciding what song I should sing at Wednesdays audition."

"How so?" he asks.

"There are at least six guys who are going to audition for probably three or four solo slots. I'm sure some of those guys are going to be getting their friends in the choir to listen to them sing an audition piece at this rehearsal and to critique their singing. I'd really like to ask Keira or maybe one of the tenors who isn't auditioning to listen to me sing my piece."

"Have you picked a song?"

"I'm going to do that tonight."

"Maybe I can help you."

Maybe he could. I hadn't thought about that. But I still want a reason to go to Saturday's rehearsal, so I say, "Yeah. That would be great. How about on Tuesday night, after I've picked a piece and tried it out on Saturday."

"Will there be adults at this rehearsal?"

Oh no, answering this question could kill the whole deal. I know Kelly told me that the section leads would be leading the rehearsal. The school can't require students to meet outside of regular school hours, except for designated programs, like our fall program. And Mrs. Walker can't formally schedule a Saturday rehearsal or officially lead one. But in the past, she has shown up and played audience.

Anyway, I need to soft pedal the "adults-on-hand" thing. "The section leads will run the rehearsal, but Mrs. Walker always attends," I tell him. That's sorta true.

"And Angela's mother will be there."

Now I'm pushing the truth envelope a bit. I'm not sure Mrs. Potter will be there, but I'd be surprised if she wasn't somewhere in the house.

"So there will be adult supervision." Dad pauses as if he's expecting me to say something else or at least clarify, but I don't. "What time is the rehearsal?" he says finally.

"From one to four in the afternoon."

Dad shakes his head. Is that a "yes" shake, or a "no" shake? I can't tell.

"Will there be food at this rehearsal?" he asks.

"Probably pizza." Then I anticipate his next question and add, "but no alcohol. It really is a rehearsal. Just a little more informal than our regular Wednesday meetings." To seal the deal, I tell him it's team-building for the choir: "We get to know the new choir members. Almost a third of the choir this year is new. And almost everyone in the choir will be there."

There's a pause. Dad is big on team-building. He is constantly talking about how things might have been better at the UW if his department had worked together more as a team. I know he supports me being in the choir. He encouraged me to try out to solo last year. So I can tell that he's considering what I've said.

"OK, sounds fine, but I'll want to drive you there."

He's agreeing that I can go. This is great! Then I unexpectedly think about Toby. I see her face just like I did that morning when she woke me up to go out to the island.

"Wake up, Robin."

I shake my head and her image fades. She's not here. I know she's not here. She's . . . I've got to quit thinking about this. What happened really wasn't my fault. I've got important things to do. I've got to stay focused. If I stay focused, I'll be OK. All I want is for everything to get back to normal.

"You OK?" Dad asks.

"Yeah, just spacing a bit." I pull myself together, smile and say, "Thanks."

CHAPTER FIFTEEN

The Singing Party

I had always thought that deciding on an audition song would be fun. But with the rehearsal party coming up tomorrow and the solo auditions on Wednesday, I have to scramble to decide what I'm going to sing. Turns out it's much harder than I thought it would be.

Another problem is this odd voice hoarseness I've been experiencing, particularly in the morning and when I sing. Luckily, it's not that noticeable at rehearsals. I can sing a little softer, so my voice gets kind of covered up by the sound of the other tenors. But other people are starting to notice. Dixon took me aside after the second rehearsal and suggested I try using a nasal inhaler. I guess he'd heard something he didn't like.

After Dad and I eat, I head up to my room to look through the songbook and think about potential solo audition songs. I could probably sing half the songs in the songbook, but I have to pick songs that I already know. I don't have time to learn a new song. And it's got to be in my range—I'm a second tenor so it can't be too high or very low. And it can't be too slow, or too old fashioned. Finally, there is a lot of popular music that is identified with girl singers, so those songs are also out.

I pick twelve possible songs from the songbook to start with, and then begin cutting down the list. "Shenandoah" (too old and slow), "The Girls of Summer," and "Morning Morgan Town" (too girly) go first, although I wonder about "Shenandoah." It certainly would show off my voice. But it might really tax it too. I love Kurt Weill's "Lost in the Stars," but I don't know the music well enough to sing it without considerable practice. I expect some of the basses, especially George Little, will be singing something from *Carousel* or *Oklahoma*, so I drop "Oh, What a Beautiful Morning" off my list. That's too bad because it's another big showy piece. But I can't stop worrying that I'll end up singing the same song as either Dixon or George at the audition, and that would be terrible because they've got the best male voices in the choir, although this new guy Phinney might challenge them for that title.

Now I'm down to five songs: "A Fellow Needs a Girl," "Forever Young," "Some Enchanted Evening," "They Call the Wind Mariah," and "Tonight" from *West Side Story*. I can't decide on just one, so I go downstairs and show the list to Dad.

"Let's have you run through each song," he says.

I sound fine on "A Fellow Needs a Girl." But the song seems kind of slight, and I feel like I need something that I can sing with more energy to really grab Mrs. Walker's attention. I love Dylan's "Forever Young," but I can tell by the time I'm through singing it that right now the really high parts are too much for my voice. The other three songs sound fine, although by the time I'm through singing "They Call the Wind Mariah," my throat feels real scratchy, even a little sore.

"So what do you think?" I ask Dad.

"I think we need to get you a nasal inhaler tomorrow and have you use it every day before your audition. I wonder if you've got an allergy to something?"

"I mean about the songs. Which songs should I concentrate on?"

"I'd just pick one. Pick the one you feel the strongest about. If you're unsure just pick one. You can try it out tomorrow and see what you think."

I head back up to my room and mull over which of the three songs would be best to use. The one I like the best is "They Call the Wind Mariah," but if my voice is scratchy on Wednesday, Mrs. Walker will certainly hear that with this song. "Some Enchanted Evening" feels like a safer choice. It's well within my range, but it's slow. "Tonight" might be the best of the three because it's showier and still within my range. Still I can't decide. I'm vacillating between the three songs, and I'm too tired to decide anything tonight.

Before I can get into bed, I email Mike. He responds with the usual "what's happening" and "I'm counting on hearing you at the holiday concert." Then I ask about his "big surprise," expecting him to say something about his family or his college applications. But it turns out he has a girlfriend:

You know that girl you saw me talking to in the library the week before school started? She's in my AP Biology class and we've started hanging out together.

Dude! Does this mean you're officially dating?

I wait for Mike's reply. Being a babe magnet has its problems, Mike's constantly getting asked out. But he's never really hung out steadily with any particular girl. Girls weren't a priority, maybe because with his good looks, he knew they would be around when the time was right. When his message finally shows up on my screen, I chuckle as I read what Mike wrote:

We started meeting at that coffee place, the one a couple blocks from school, and we've been to a couple movies.

I write back:

Wow, you've taken this chick to the movies. Twice! Sounds like you're hooked, dude.

Nancy's pretty smart. In fact, she's kind of a math genius. She's fun to talk to. I can tell her about the Burgess Shale and all the extinctions, and she can explain the idea of proofs. She likes movies, too.

A math genius, huh? Well that explains everything. Glad to know it doesn't have anything to do with her being so hot.

Yeah, she's pretty hot too. Don't you think?

I guess. Have things got hot and heavy yet?

Mike's response is slow in coming. Despite his good looks, Mike sometimes seems uncomfortable talking too much about girls. I know that his family is, if anything, more determined than he is to see that he gets into a good college. So even after he got to high school, he was forbidden to date until he was a junior. His parents did encourage him to get involved in social activities, like dances and clubs at school, and they let him invite girls home to study and work on school projects. He was on the junior prom planning committee, and he took Sara Chin to the prom. But they were never a real item.

Well, a little, maybe.

Maybe? It either has or it hasn't.

What can I say? You know. Anyway, she's smart and good-looking, and she's tons of fun too hang out with. So eat your heart out, Robbie Hood.

Don't get too interested, man. Remember you'll be going off to college next fall.

Yeah, I know.

I can tell Mike's getting tired of this topic, and I'm feeling exhausted myself after struggling all day to pick an audition song. Mike wishes me good luck with the rehearsal party, then adds:

Catch me after AP Environmental Science on Tuesday? Nancy's in that class, and I'll formally introduce you.

Great.

I sleep like a baby, and when I wake up, I notice I'm not hoarse. But I'm still undecided about which song to try out at today's rehearsal party. I practice singing all three up in my room before I go downstairs, and all three sound fine or at least OK. For a moment I think maybe I should try "Moon River," but it's too late to add anything else to the mix of songs I'm considering. So I'm still debating what to sing as I leave for the party.

I have my license, but there has never been any real talk about me getting a car. I'm supposed to negotiate with Dad about using our old Toyota, the family's second car, and the one Dad usually drives to work. That has never worked very well. And now, of course, it's not really a topic I can bring up. Driving privileges are for good boys. So today Dad drives me to the rehearsal party at Angela's.

Her house is big—not one of those mega mansions that everybody hates so much, but still pretty big. Angela's mother greets everyone at the door. She's apparently keen to meet all the choir members as they show up. She seems nice enough.

Mrs. Potter directs everybody down a hallway to a big recreation room, where someone has pushed a pool table and comfortable chairs to one side and set up a riser for the choir. It looks like most of the choir has shown up.

Kelly greets me with a big hug as I walk into the rec room. "Robin, it's great you could come." She gives me her usual happy Kelly smile, which seems even brighter today, and for some reason I find it a little embarrassing.

But I just say, "Yeah, I'm glad Dad let me come. I was afraid they wouldn't let me out of house arrest for anything that sounded like it would be the least bit fun. But I talked my Dad into it."

"I'm sorry things are so tough for you at home," Kelly says, obviously trying to show as much empathy as she can.

Across the room I see Keira talking with Angela and a small group of other girls. She waves at me and then goes back to talking.

"Yeah, luckily Mom went back to Maine."

Kelly looks confused for a minute, but then responds, "Well, anyway I'm glad you were able to come."

There's an awkward moment or two when neither of us quite knows what to say. Then Phinney taps me on the shoulder. "Hey, Robin. Ready to sing?"

"That's why I'm here." I turn around, and Phinney and I walk over to where Dixon is standing. "See you later," I say over my shoulder to Kelly.

Now everybody is milling around, talking about school, or what he or she will be doing over the weekend. But before it gets too loud, Angela stands up and welcomes everybody. I notice her mom standing just inside the door at the back of the room, keeping her eye on things, I guess.

As Angela sits down, Keira stands up and says, "Anybody who hasn't brought their music—there are copies of the four songs we'll be singing on the table to the left of the risers."

"OK, let's get organized and sing," George Little says in his booming bass voice.

At our regular rehearsals, it sometimes gets pretty loud before everybody gets settled on the risers. But today everybody seems relaxed, not stressed or exhausted like after a day at school. So it doesn't take folks long to find their spot.

As everybody's getting settled, Dixon announces that anybody planning to audition to solo, who wants feedback from other singers, can practice their solos in the room next door after the main rehearsal at about 3:00.

"And don't forget there will be pizza and soda in the dining room starting at 3:00," Angela says. "And if you need water, there's bottled water on the table by the music."

Boy, Angela and her mother have thought of everything.

We're just getting into our first song when Mrs. Walker walks in and sits down by Mrs. Potter. She pulls out a little notebook, as if she's planning to take notes about what she hears. The atmosphere gets a little more serious when the singers realize she's in the room.

The rehearsal goes well. The four section leads take turns leading the choir. I know Dixon plans to major in choral conducting at UW, so this is just practice for him. We sing through all four songs. There are a few rough spots, but nothing we can't correct. More important for me, I don't notice any real problems with my voice. But when we stop for a short break at 2:00, I notice a little tickle in my throat, so I head for the music table to get a water bottle.

Dixon, George, and Phinney are standing together in a small circle, talking. I wonder if they're talking about the solo auditions, so I walk over. It turns out I'm right.

"Is Mrs. Walker staying for the solo rehearsal?" Phinney asks.

"She's already gone," Dixon says, and he nods over to the door.

I turn and glance in that direction. Some folks are leaving the room to head for the bathroom or to talk outside. Mrs. Potter is talking to some singers by the door. But Dixon's right: the chair Mrs. Walker was sitting in is now empty.

"So, have you guys decided what you're going to sing for the auditions?" Dixon asks.

George nods his head, "Probably, 'Oh, What a Beautiful Morning.'"

I knew it, something from *Oklahoma*. Then Phinney says, "I'm thinking of doing 'Grace,' an Irish love song."

That's a surprise. It's not a song I recognize. That could be risky for Phinney since Mrs. Walker may not have heard it either and won't know what to expect.

"What about you, Steele?" George asks.

"I'm not a hundred percent sure. It's between 'Tonight,' 'They Call the Wind Mariah,' and 'Some Enchanted Evening.'"

"Ah, show tunes. Good old standards, if a bit conservative," says Dixon.

I immediately wonder if he's trying to mess with my mind.

"So, are you going to practice anything today?" Dixon asks.

Now my mind is scrambling to decide which of the three songs I should try. But before I can answer, Marcus Jackson joins the group.

"Did I hear someone say that they were going to sing 'They Call the Wind Mariah'?" he says.

I nod my head. "Yeah."

"Well, I'm just letting you know that I'm planning on using that as my audition song."

Well, that narrows the field. There's not a rule that says two people can't sing the same song at an audition. But going head-to-head with another singer could be a problem. Best not to try it. Maybe I shouldn't sing anything today if I'm so undecided. But no, that doesn't feel right either.

We get back together for another forty give-or-take minutes. While I'm singing again with the group, I come to a decision. My voice sounds clear again after the break, and I decide I'll sing "Tonight" at today's solo practice.

As it turns out, we end up practicing our solos in the rec room because it's the only room with a piano. The girls go first, but only two girls actually sing: Shannon Cooper and Monique Jackson, Marcus's sister.

Keira doesn't sing, but she lets everyone know she's planning to sing "Memory" from *Cats* at her audition. She'll sound great, and I doubt anyone will even come close to challenging her for best solo auditioning performance.

Then it's the guys' turn. Marcus Jackson sings "They Call the Wind Mariah," and his voice sounds strong. Still, I think mine is more melodic, at least when I'm singing my best. Dixon surprises everyone when he doesn't sing. He says he's practicing at home, but I wonder what song he's chosen.

George sings "Oh What a Beautiful Morning." His voice is perfect for that song. Then I sing "Tonight." I sound fine, except for a little crack in my voice right at the end. But somehow it feels uninspired.

Finally, Phinney sings "Grace." Wow! It turns out to be a sad love song about an IRA prisoner waiting to be executed, who writes a song for the wife he'll never be able to see again. A great choice of material, and Phinney sings it perfectly. For a moment, after he stops, we all seem a little dazed. Then everyone crowds around Phinney complimenting him and asking him questions about the song.

"Nicely done," says Dixon.

It's a tradition not to applaud at rehearsals, but George and Marcus raise their hands and high-five Phinney, who seems a little embarrassed by all the attention.

With Phinney the center of attention, nobody says anything to me about "Tonight." I guess that's OK. Phinney's performance took everybody by surprise, but I suspect I wasn't outstanding enough for anybody to really notice.

"What a beautiful song," I tell Phinney. "How did you learn it?"

"My father taught it to me," says Phinney. "He called it a *Go ha'lainn* song."

"A what song?" asks Marcus.

"*Go ha'lainn* is Irish for beautiful or lovely."

By now everybody who stayed around to sing or listen has headed toward the dining room and the pizza. I feel a little dejected. I thought I sounded fine for the practice, but probably not good enough if this had been the actual solo audition.

As if to reinforce that feeling, Dixon walks up beside me and say, "A lot of competition this year to sing solos."

I know that. Is he just trying to make me nervous?

"Yeah," I say, trying to sound as casual as I can. But he's right, what with Phinney sounding so good and with at least two or three other tenors, including Dixon, likely to audition. This year's solo competition looks really tough.

"You might want to consider a different song."

I slow down and glance at Dixon. Is he serious? Does he hope I'll panic and decide not to audition?

"Try finding a song you can sing with a little more passion."

"OK . . . thanks," I say, not sounding very sincere. I feel a little broadsided by Dixon's comment. But then I think, *maybe he's right*

As we get closer to the dining room, we can smell the pizza.

"Well, I'm going to go get some of that pizza before it's all gone," Dixon says with a smile. "I'll see you on Wednesday." He picks up his pace and joins George, Phinney, and Marcus, who are just ahead of us. I lag behind, trying to decide what I'm going to do about an audition song.

The dining room is crowded with singers. I grab myself two slices from the last box of pizza, and then try to find a place to sit. After a minute, I notice someone waving at me from the other side of the room. It's Kelly. She's somehow been able to save me a spot by her and a couple of her girlfriends. Do I want to go sit with them? I glance around to see if there are any open spots with some of the guys, but Kelly seems to have the only open and available space in the dining room. I could go stand in the hall with the four or five introverts in the choir, who never seem to hang with anybody, but that would just be too depressing.

I walk over to Kelly, and she introduces me to two altos I've seen before but don't actually know.

"You sounded great," she says.

I saw her standing right by the door listening as the guys sang. I doubt she could tell that much about my sound from that far away.

"Thanks, but I'm thinking about trying another song."

"Why?" she asks.

"'Tonight' didn't feel right."

"I love 'Tonight,'" Kelly says.

"You just love *West Side Story*," says one of her alto friends, Alison, a sophomore with a good, but not outstanding, voice. She's pretty in a fragile sort of way.

Kelly smiles and says, "Yeah, I do. But you really did sound good, Robin. Better than any of the other guys, except for maybe that new guy, Phinney."

Now I know she's exaggerating. "He did sound great, didn't he?" I say. "And I'm glad you thought I sounded ok. But I'm thinking of changing my audition song to 'Some Enchanted Evening' or maybe something else."

"Oh," says Kelly's other alto friend. "I like that song, even if it is a little slow."

"Well," Kelly says, "whatever you sing, it'll be great. You just need to have a little confidence. But I've got my fingers crossed for you, and I'm betting you'll get picked. I think this is your year to solo, Robin Steele."

"I wish I was so sure." I glance at my watch. If I had a cell phone, I wouldn't need to have a watch. It's 4:15. "I've got to finish and get out front. My Dad's picking me up." I wolf down one last piece of pizza and stand up to go. "See you ladies at rehearsal on Wednesday." I nod to Kelly, who smiles back at me.

Allison and the other girl both nod.

"Bye Robin," Kelly says. "Break a leg on Wednesday." That's a theater term for good luck. Kelly's in the West High Players, and I think her first love is acting.

I can tell she wants to say something else, but I'm in a hurry to go. I need to talk with Dad about the rehearsal and about finding another song because I've got to sound better at my audition on Wednesday. I'll practice hard the next three days and then sing "Some Enchanted Evening," or maybe something else. I'm still not sure what.

Chapter Sixteen

Hearing Voices

When I'm in my room lying on the bed daydreaming about being in the field digging up fossils or listening to music on my headphones, Moon Pie will sometimes jump up on the bed and climb onto my chest while I'm partially lost in one of these dreams. She'll close her eyes, and start purring. That's when I hear, "*Look, Robbie!*"

I open my eyes, and, of course, nobody is there. But I can feel a presence. Then I remember how Toby would come into my room on some Saturday mornings and yell at me to get up because we had something to do or somewhere to go. Often, she'd have Moon Pie under one arm, the cat looking like she was going to be sick. I remember her interrupting me while I was doing homework to tell me how Moon Pie had brought a dead bird or mouse into the house. So, since Moon Pie had been a bad kitty, Toby was leaving her in my room all night as punishment. Then, before I could object, she'd drop Moon Pie on the bed and stomp out.

When I think about those things, I realize how much Toby loved Moon Pie. She treated the cat like a little sister, carting her around, alternately talking to her, lecturing her, and pampering her. No matter how irritating Toby is, I have to admire the way she loves that cat. Yes, she can be really annoying, but she is my sister, and now she's missing and maybe even dead. And I was the last one to see her, and I still can't figure out what happened.

"Toby, where are you?" There is no answer.

"Probably the biggest idea you need to grasp when studying environmental science is that large-scale creation and destruction are the major forces in the geological history of Earth." Mrs. Daniels looks around class on Monday to make sure everyone is listening. Despite the droopy-eyed, half-asleep look on many of the students' faces, everybody is looking right at the teacher. Most of these kids want to be in this class. The others know that they need the class—and a good grade—to get into a college of their choice.

"So, give me some examples of what I'm talking about."

Immediately, kids start waving their hands.

"Volcanoes," a guy says from the other side of the room.

"Correct, Mr. Nelson. But wait until you're called on next time," Mrs. Daniels says. "Yes, volcanoes are probably one of the most obvious examples. Ms. Graham." She nods at Lindsey Graham, a cheerleader type with a brain to match her bod.

"Earthquakes and tsunamis," Lindsey says.

"Yes, Ms. Graham."

The number of hands remaining in the air drops a bit. After a pause, Mrs. Daniels turns and calls on me.

"Mr. Steele."

"Mountain building."

"Correct, Mr. Steele. And mountain building is a part of what larger process that has completely changed Earth's landforms over millions of years?"

"Plate tectonics," I say, without waiting for Mrs. Daniels to give me a nod to keep going.

"Yes! And remember, everyone, please wait until you are recognized to give an answer."

Mrs. Daniels is a stickler for making sure everyone gets a chance to participate. But still it's the aggressive kids, like Mike and me, who end up answering most of the questions.

"Plate tectonics has been the biggest factor changing landforms over the life of the Earth. This includes mountain building, earthquakes, and most volcanism."

Only a few hands remain raised.

"Any other examples?" Mrs. Daniels asks.

Quickly she looks over at Mike. He's been waiting patiently with his hand up since the beginning of Mrs. Daniels' Q & A session.

"Mr. Sakoda."

"Sea level rise caused by global warming."

"Yes, and we might just say *climate change* because extreme climate change has been a factor in a number of the catastrophic events that have affected the earth over its life. So, those events are?"

About five of us immediately raise our hands.

"Ms. O'Neill."

Shelly O'Neill is a quiet, mousy girl, who seldom volunteers to speak. But today she does because, I suspect, she knows the right answer.

"The major extinctions."

"Correct. And thank you, Ms. O'Neill. Earth has suffered many catastrophic events in its 13.7-billion-year history. Early in its life, Earth had long periods of volcanism. Glaciers covered much of Earth at different times, the most spectacular of these being about 650 million years ago, when glaciers may have reached clear to the equator. Since then, the earth has suffered smaller ice ages about every one hundred thousand years. The last of these lasted until about fifteen thousand years ago.

"These events changed the climate and resulted in species extinctions. In fact, Earth has seen multiple periods of species extinction throughout its life. Some of these relate to plate tectonics, the breakup and merging of continents, others to catastrophic events such as extensive volcanism, or Earth being hit by a comet or asteroid. But the direct cause of most extinctions has been climate change and habitat disruption."

Mrs. Daniels stops and moves to a PowerPoint projector she has set up. A mosaic of pictures appears on the screen. There are objects crashing into Earth, volcanoes erupting, the atmosphere turning smoky and brown, dinosaurs and large marine animals and coral reefs dying. What could they do? Nothing, nothing but die.

Then I immediately think about Toby and I wonder—what can we do? Nothing either, it seems.

"Scientists have determined that Earth has had five great extinctions. Who can name all five?"

About half of the class raises their hands. I'm a little surprised when she calls on Nancy Folger, Mike's new honey. Mike keeps saying Nancy's "really smart." But I can only remember her answering a few fairly easy questions in class. Still Nancy has changed my life in one big way. I haven't seen much of Mike since he started hanging out with her. Even the email between us has dropped way off.

"The Ordovician, Devonian, Late Permian . . ." Nancy pauses.

It's obvious she's having trouble remembering number four. It's the one that kind of gets lost because the one that has captured everyone's imagination is the big fifth extinction, the K-T that killed off the dinosaurs.

"The Cretaceous-Tertiary Extinction is the fifth," she says after a minute. "And was the fourth the Jurassic?"

"OK, class. Ms. O'Neill has named four of the five major extinction events. Who can name the missing fourth event?"

Again hands shoot up.

"OK, those of you with your hands up give your classmates the correct name."

"The Late Triassic," about eight of us say all at once.

"So what characterizes a major extinction?"

More hands. Mrs. Daniels nods in my direction. "Mr. Steele."

"The extinction of at least seventy-five percent of the species on Earth at the time of the event."

"Yes, and so why is understanding these great extinction events especially important to us today?"

Only five hands go up immediately. And the most prominent among them is Mike's. He's obviously got an answer he wants to give.

"OK, Mr. Sakoda."

"Scientists think we are at the beginning of a sixth great extinction event caused by global warming."

"Yes," says Mrs. Daniels. "Current projections are that if the planet continues to warm at its current rate, and humans continue to destroy habitat at the current rate, seventy-five percent of mammal species currently alive will become extinct in about three hundred years.

"Your assignment for Thursday is to study one of the five great extinctions and to be prepared to talk about that event in class. Since there are fifteen of you, I'm going to break you into five groups of three people apiece."

She divides us into groups by counting off one, two, three, four, five. I'm in group four. Mike's in group three. The other two people in group four are Lindsay Graham and Nancy Folger. My group is to report on the Late Triassic Extinction. This is really short notice to research and write a report. Given the fact that I've got a solo audition on Wednesday, I'll have to spend tonight looking at websites and trying to take notes.

"Do we need to turn in a written report Thursday on our research?" someone asks.

"No, I know this is short notice. So I'm not asking you to write a report. But you'll want to take good notes on your assigned extinction and on what's said in class on Thursday. This is to be an in-class sharing of information. But we might—we probably will—come back to it later in the class. So please be prepared."

She's letting us know that something about extinctions will be on the final exam.

"You can use websites, but make sure the sites you use are authoritative science sites or science journals sites. Now get together and plan your research."

Students shuffle around to get together in their groups. Nancy smiles when I say hi. It bothers me a little that Mike has never introduced us. But she seems friendly enough. Lindsay is all business. She wants us to exchange email addresses so that we can share any good websites or other sources we find. That makes sense. I just wonder when I'm going to get time to do the research. But I decide not to mention the audition. I doubt I'd get much sympathy from overachievers like Nancy and Lindsay.

As class ends, Mike comes over to get Nancy. We haven't gotten together to study after school for two weeks. I could use his help in getting organized on this extinction project. So I ask, "Do you want to get together at my place for a while after school to talk about this project? I'm kinda swamped this week and need to do a lot of my research tonight."

"Gee, Robbie, I can't. I'm having dinner at Nancy's, and we're going to study together at her place. But I'll email you later."

I must look unhappy with Mike's response. Anyway, he shrugs and I can tell he's feeling a little uncomfortable.

"Even better since Nancy is in your group. She can let you know what we come up via email."

"I was planning to do that, Robin," Nancy says.

"Sure," I say.

"You don't text?" Nancy asks.

"No, I don't have a phone."

Nancy looks a little confused, but then she smiles. "That's OK. I've got your email address, so I'll just email you."

We walk out into the hall together. It's really crowded, with about half the kids going to or coming back from lunch, while the others are just milling around, talking, and slowly making their way to their lockers or to class.

Mike and Nancy turn to head toward the cafeteria. Then Nancy glances back over her shoulder. "Want to join us at lunch?"

I feel awkward and uncomfortable. Mike essentially just blew me off about getting together to study. He knows how important it is to me to do well in AP Environmental Science. But obviously he's hot and heavy into Nancy. So, I'm not feeling too sociable right now. "No, thanks, I've got to spend lunch in the library. With my audition coming up on Wednesday, I've got to get a head start looking up information for our report."

When I get to the library it is almost empty. I sit down at a computer terminal. But before I can type in anything, I hear that voice again. The voice I hear sometimes when I'm alone in my room, Toby's voice.

"Wake up, Robbie. Wake up."

CHAPTER SEVENTEEN

The Audition

By the time I get home, I'm frantic. I go straight to the computer to work on researching the Late Triassic extinction. At dinner, I can't stop telling Dad how worried I am. I don't have time to prepare for both my solo audition on Wednesday and the oral report on Thursday.

"Take things one step at a time," Dad says finally. "Let's have you sing a few of the songs you feel good about after dinner. Then we can talk about what sounds best."

So that's what we do. Unfortunately, every time I try singing right after I eat, I struggle with congestion. Dad says I probably have postnasal drip or maybe a food allergy. Ugh.

"Did you use that nasal inhaler I got you?"

"No, I forgot this morning, and again after I got home."

"Well, use it tonight before you got to bed, and again in the morning," Dad says.

But that doesn't help me tonight. I sing "Some Enchanted Evening," and my voice sounds really scratchy. Then I try "Hello Young Lovers" and "Tonight," and both sound better. When I finally try "Forever Young," it sounds the best.

I drink some water to rehydrate myself, and I sing each song a couple more times. After the second go-round, it's clear that "Some Enchanted Evening" isn't the right song to sing at the audition. But, of the other three, I'm still not sure which is best.

When I told Dad at dinner about the great reaction Phinney got when he sang that Irish ballad on Saturday, he suggests maybe I should try singing a folk song myself, something like "The Eddystone Light," or "Freeborn Man," or "Here's to You Rounders." I think "The Eddystone Light" is probably too slight a song and wouldn't impress Mrs. Walker. I'd have to work pretty hard to get "Freeborn Man" down in less than two days. But "Here's to You Rounders" might work.

Dad goes into the workroom he shares with Mom, and when he comes back, he hands me the music and lyrics for "Rounders," which he's copied from an old songbook. Then he gets his guitar to accompany me. I'll be singing *a cappella* at the audition, but for now it'll be easier if I have musical accompaniment. The song is right in my range. It's about losing someone you never got a chance to know, a grandfather, and about halfway through, I start to feel sad, almost like I'm going to cry. I stop singing, and then Dad stops playing.

"Are you all right?" he asks.

I nod my head, yes. I don't understand it myself. But one thing is for sure: I wouldn't want that to happen when I'm auditioning.

"It's a nice song, but maybe a little too sad. You know, with everything that's been going on. Anyway, I'd have to sing it while looking at the words, and I think that would be a mistake. Mrs. Walker is always talking to us about knowing the words, so we don't have to read them during a performance."

I go back and sing the other three songs one more time. But by the last song, I'm getting hoarse. "I don't know which to choose," I say. "This is going to be such a disaster."

"I think you're making this too hard. You'll sound fine whichever one you choose."

"Which one do your think sounds best?"

"Well, I'd say 'Forever Young.' For one thing, you sing it with more energy than you do the others." Dad pauses as if he's thinking about whether he should say something else. Then he adds, "I think 'Here's to You Rounders' would be a good song for your voice if you could focus on singing it and not think about other things."

I wonder what Mrs. Walker would think of my using a Bob Dylan song for my audition? She's added a lot about show tunes and ballads to our repertoire, and I'm betting she will like "Grace" when Phinney sings it at his audition. But how will she react to my using a song by such a popular American singer? I don't know. But I've got to choose a song, and I feel like I've got to do it tonight.

"OK," I say finally, "I'll go with 'Forever Young.'"

"Great. I think you'll do fine."

I can tell he's trying to give me more confidence, now that I've picked a song. But I'm still not feeling confident.

"And you'll want to practice the song again tomorrow evening. But don't overdo it. Your voice will need a rest before Wednesday."

"OK, the other thing I'm still nervous about is that I have to sing after choir practice. That means I'll be singing for an hour and then auditioning."

"Use the inhaler in the morning," Dad says. "Then take an apple and have it for lunch. Having a regular lunch would probably add to any congestion you already have. Also, drink lots of water during choir rehearsal and especially right before you sing at the audition."

As we're talking, I start to feel less anxious. I've decided on a song and I have a plan for Wednesday. For the first time, I'm feeling that I'll do OK at the audition. At least, I think I'll sing well enough that Mrs. Walker will have to consider me.

"And be sure you get a good night's sleep before the audition, and try not to worry so much."

Yes, I've got to relax if I can.

I can't remember where I first heard "Forever Young," but Dad says it was probably when we visited Bill for Grandma Helen's funeral. Mom said it was a favorite of Grandpa Bill's. He called it an anthem for the generation that came of age in the 1960s. And he said he was so glad to finally meet me that he sang the song in my honor the night after Helen's funeral. I think he liked that fact that I was a singer, and maybe he needed to sing it because it brought back happier memories.

Anyway, when we left to go home, Bill gave me a Joan Baez CD with the song on it. Later, I put it on my playlist. And I find myself singing it, or just listening to it on my player, all the time. Particularly when I need to feel strong and not afraid. I guess that's why I can sing it with such passion.

At around 9:30 I checked my email and found a message from Nancy with a list of website addresses on the Late Triassic extinction. She included a note:

Check these out and you'll probably have Thursday's assignment covered. And let me know if you find anything else you think will help us with the report. See you in class tomorrow. —NF

Quickly I check out the sites. They all look good, if a little technical. I'll have to look at these sites a little more closely tomorrow. For now, I quickly email Nancy to thank her and attach a couple of articles that I found in my rush library research at lunch. It looks like there is some controversy about the size of the Late Triassic extinction. But I can't deal with this now. I have to get to bed. Just then a notice that I've received a new email pops up on the screen.

> Hey Dude, Good luck with your solo audition on Wednesday. I know you've been sweating it, but you'll do fine. Check in with me when you get a chance after class on Thursday. —Mike

I log off the computer. Mike still hasn't acknowledged that he ignored me when I asked him to help me with my report. But the way the evening went, I really needed the time to sing and to decide on the song to sing at my audition. Anyway, I'm glad I've made my decision. Now I really need to get to bed.

I must be feeling more relaxed because I go right to sleep after I hit the pillow. Then, somewhere around 4:00 a.m., I hear Toby's voice again, saying, "Wake up Robin!"

I feel what seems like a sea breeze and shake myself awake. I've got to be dreaming. The room is dark and totally silent. It's all in my head. But still, I can't go back to sleep. I lie there listening for the voice but hearing nothing, until the room fills with bird song. I look at my watch—it's 5:30.

I sleepwalk through much of Tuesday. When Lindsay, Nancy, and I meet for ten minutes right after AP Environmental Sciences, I mostly listen. Then we divide up the report, with each of us taking responsibility for presenting a part. Mrs. Daniels wants every student to present something when we do oral reports.

I practice "Forever Young" twice after Dad gets home. He says I sound great, but I'm too tired to judge. After dinner, I pick up the music for "Here's to You Rounders," which I see lying on an end table in the living room. Back in my room, I lie down on the bed and find myself looking at that song. It's very sad but also beautiful. I try slowly singing it through, but again I feel myself starting to cry. Maybe, I'm too tired to do anything more tonight but sleep. Before I go to bed, I stuff the music for "Rounders" into my backpack.

Wednesday drags by although I feel more rested. When I get to practice, I open my backpack to pull out the songbook I'd taken from the stack Mrs. Walker had left for people planning to audition. I notice the music for "Rounders" at the back of the pack, and I pull it out, thinking I'll toss it into the wastepaper basket. But then I'm interrupted. It's Kiera. She's come over to wish me luck with my audition. I stuff the "Rounders" music into my shirt pocket and put my backpack on a chair under my coat.

The choir members scramble to find their place on the risers. Then Mrs. Walker asks those planning to audition to raise their hands. I glance around quickly to see if I can count the guys who raise their hands. I see seven, I think. She writes down the names in alphabetical order. The girls will go first and then the guys. That means I'll be the last to audition.

Finally, Mrs. Walker goes down her list, asking each person what he or she plans to sing. Getting to the guys, she calls on Dixon first. My heart jumps when he says "Forever Young." Suddenly I'm disoriented and have to catch myself so I don't stumble off the risers. We can't sing the same song. Even if Mrs. Walker would let us, I can't be in direct competition with Dixon. Next, she asks Alan Brooks, but I'm so panicked that I don't hear what Alan is going to sing. All I can think about is what am I going to sing?

Mrs. Walker calls the next person's name, but now I'm not paying attention. What were the names of the songs I practiced? The only ones I can remember are "Some Enchanted Evening" and "Forever Young." One song I'd decided not to sing and one I can't sing because someone else is singing it. Then I remember "Tonight." That would be easy. I know I can sing it, but will it get me a solo? Then I remember the music in my shirt pocket, and I pull out "Here's to You Rounders."

Do I remember enough of this song to get by without having to look at the lyrics?

Mrs. Walker calls George Little's name. I'm running out of time. I have to make a decision. Since I'll be the last person to audition, maybe I can sneak out for a few minutes before I have to sing, find an empty classroom, and practice.

"Mr. Steele."

I stare down at the lyrics for "Rounders." I can remember the first, third and last verses and the chorus. If I can somehow get the second verse down, I'll be OK.

"Mr. Steele," Mrs. Walker says again.

She's calling my name. I have to choose, and either way that means taking a chance. But "Rounders" will sound better, I think. I hope. Anyway, I'm dropping "Tonight."

"Here's to You Rounders," I say.

Mrs. Walker looks a little confused, and I realize she doesn't know the song.

"It's a modern folk song," I say.

She nods her head and writes the name down on her list.

"OK, singers. For those of you who are auditioning, auditions will start at 3:15. I'd like everyone else to leave the auditorium before the auditions start."

I may have caught a break. I'll have fifteen minutes to practice, or at least look over the words after choir practice ends.

"And anyone who is auditioning needs to be back in this room when we start the auditions. Oh, and one more thing: I'll post the names of this school year's soloists on the bulletin board outside my office Friday afternoon."

I get another break when Mrs. Walker dismisses the choir at 2:55. I rush out of the auditorium and find an empty classroom just down the hall. I go through the song three times. I've got it, I think.

Then I glance at my watch—*3:14!*—and bound out of the room and back to the auditorium. I can hardly remember what happens over the next forty minutes. I do remember hearing Keira sing "Midnight." I thought she was outstanding. But mostly I kept glancing at the lyrics for "Here's to You Rounders" and taking swigs out of my water bottle to keep my voice as clear as possible.

Finally, Mrs. Walker calls my name. I walk up to the piano and when she nods her head, I start to sing. I sing my heart out, stumbling a little on the rhythm of the third line of verse three, but I keep going, and then I'm through.

When I'm through, I stand there for a minute. The room is very quiet. Then gradually the other kids get up, pick up their backpacks and book bags and start to leave.

I look over at Mrs. Walker. She's writing some notes in her small notebook. The auditions are over. Now all we can do is wait for Friday to find out whom she picks.

I walk over to my seat and pick up my backpack. I put the music for "Here's to You Rounders" back in my backpack.

"A surprising choice, Steele," Dixon says as he walks by. He's smiling, but I can't tell if he liked my singing or he just liked the song.

"Nice song, Robin," someone else says. It's Phinney. He stops beside me. "It sounds a lot like the traditional Irish music I grew up with—powerful and sad."

"My Mom and Dad are both singers," I say. "I grew up listening to folk music."

"Same with me," says Phinney. "My grandfather sang in pubs for years. So I grew up hearing and singing traditional Irish music."

"So did mine before he became a minister."

We are both smiling when we walk out of the auditorium. I'm feeling more relaxed and even confident. If Phinney liked my singing, others probably did, too.

CHAPTER EIGHTEEN

Shifting Gears

Dad can't believe it when I tell him what happened. "Gutsy," he says. "That could have been a disaster if you hadn't made the right choice. How do you feel about it?"

"Kinda good and kinda glad it's over. I think I sang OK. I didn't break down and my voice sounded fine. I stumbled a bit on the third verse, but I kept going."

"Well, whatever happens, I know you gave it your best shot."

I know I did, but I see now that I took a risk. When Dad said that changing songs at the last minute could have turned out to be a disaster, I immediately thought of Toby and how even little things—what you do or don't do—can have tremendous consequences.

Mrs. Daniels says that is what's happening with us today with regard to climate change. What we aren't doing, what we're ignoring, is going to have a big impact on future generations.

Unfortunately for Lindsay, Nancy and me, what's known as the Late Triassic or Triassic/Jurassic Boundary

Extinction is the least well understood extinction, and the one about which there is the most conjecture. I didn't get much time to search the web for additional resources. But I read the article links Nancy had sent me. Most are pretty technical. Still, I get the general idea of how the extinction is seen by scientists. But now it's 10:00 p.m. and I'm exhausted. So that's all I can do tonight.

I wake up early on Thursday. I'm still tired, but I'm thinking again about Toby. So I get dressed, eat a quick breakfast, and ask Dad to drive me to school. That way, I can use the school library again before class. If nothing else, this will help me get focused on the report.

When you give a report in Mrs. Daniels's class, it's important to take a position and argue that position. That's what Mrs. D. likes to hear. She says that's how she knows we are really thinking about the material. Also, each group gets just fifteen minutes to present their report, which means you have to be able to develop a clear thesis, condense the information on your particular extinction, and then pick out and present only the material necessary to give the class a clear idea of what happened, its causes and its results.

Lindsay and Nancy are waiting for me when I get to the AP Environmental Science classroom. They must have been the first kids to arrive for class.

Scientists have put forward several explanations for the Late Triassic extinction. Some argue that there were really two extinctions: the one that caused the decline in marine invertebrates and the one responsible for the extinction of land vertebrates and plants. But to make our case as clear and as strong as possible, we'll argue that the major cause of this extinction was a massive increase in volcanism caused by the rifting of the Pangea supercontinent. This seems to be what most scientists believe.

We divide up the material, and by the time class starts, we are as prepared as we can be. When it's our turn, Lindsay presents our major thesis: that intense basalt eruptions about 200,000 years ago caused a major extinction affecting 76 percent of all life on Earth.

I then develop this idea by talking about how the increased greenhouse effect—the increased levels of atmospheric carbon dioxide, sulfur, and methane caused by the eruptions—resulted in the acidification of the oceans and a rise in the air temperature, primary causes of the die-off of most families and species.

Nancy follows me. She talks about some of the important species, like the jawless eel-like vertebrate named the conodont that died off in the Late Triassic. She also mentions how the extinction of many vertebrate species opened up environmental niches that allowed the dinosaurs to take over in the period that followed the Triassic, the Jurassic.

Finally, Lindsay argues that some of the other popular ideas about what caused the Late Triassic extinction, like the asteroid impact theory, are not supported by evidence, and that others, like climate change, were likely the result of the increase in greenhouse gases caused by rift zone volcanism.

There aren't many questions after we give our report. I think that means we scored big, and Mrs. Daniels seems to confirm that when she says, "Good, well-outlined report."

"One thing we should all take away from your report on the Late Triassic extinction is a better understanding of how science works. We don't have all the answers yet about what caused this major extinction. But scientists are working to get better geological information, and probably in the next few years, we'll have a clearer picture about what exactly caused the Late Triassic die-off.

"One thing we do know is that volcanism played some part in three of the major extinctions. Each has been mentioned today. Which are they?"

About half the class immediately raises their hands.

"OK," says Mrs. D. "Rather than have three people answer, I'm going to call on one person, and I'm hoping that person will know the right periods."

Everybody wants a shot at answering this rather easy question. But Mrs. D. quickly calls on Nancy. Naturally, she gets the answer right.

"They're the Permian, Triassic, and K-T extinctions," Nancy says.

When class ends, Nancy and Lindsay come by my desk, and we do a group high-five.

"We were great," Lindsay says. "I'm sure we aced it."

"Well, we covered all the major points," I say, trying to sound modest, but really feeling like I'd dodged a bullet and probably picked up a good grade on a report I would have really struggled to put together on my own.

Nancy smiles, and I wonder if she's thinking what I've been thinking—that we're lucky we had less material to review, talk about, and organize. I think the people who had to report on the Late Devonian and Permian extinctions had a tougher job because they had so much more information to pick through.

"Anyway," says Lindsay, "I'll work with you guys anytime." With that she tosses her head to the side, smiles, and heads for her next class.

"Nice answer to that question on volcanism," I say as Nancy and I walk out of the classroom. "You probably got some points with Mrs. Daniels for that answer."

"Do you think it's that easy to make points with Mrs. Daniels?"

"Well . . ." I say equivocally as I shake my head. It sounds like she's irritated by what I thought would be a compliment and I'm, not sure how to respond. So I punt: "Are you especially interested in geology or environmental science, or are you just trying to pile up AP classes to help you get into college?"

"Just trying to pile up AP classes for my transcript," Nancy says.

She's smiling and I can tell she's being sarcastic. I can see what why Mike likes her. She's smart and she's got this funny, mischievous smile.

"Well, actually, I want to be an environmental scientist, so taking this class is sort of a must. What about you?" she asks.

"I want to be a paleontologist."

"Just like Mike."

"Yeah, that's how we became friends. We started talking about fossils and how exciting it would be to dig up dinosaur bones, or discover a new prehistoric animal or even a plant. That's when we realized we both wanted to be paleontologists."

"So you want to go to Yale, too?"

"Actually, Berkeley, but I'll probably have to settle for UW or Western initially. Maybe after two years I can transfer. But my goal is to do my graduate work at Berkeley. What about you? How'd you get interested in the environment?"

"I've always been interested in nature, for as long as I can remember. My parents took me hiking for the first time when I was six. After that, I was hooked on everything that had to do with nature. I put up bird feeders in our yard. I joined the Audubon Society's Young Naturalist program and started reading everything I could about nature."

I like her enthusiasm and energy.

"In middle school, I learned about climate change, and I joined Plant for the Planet," she adds.

"Don't they plant trees?"

"Yes, we plant trees to help capture CO_2. We have planted trees all over the county. So anyway, I'll probably go to the University of Washington. My goal is to become either a forest scientist or a marine biologist, and UW has good programs in both."

Nancy is interesting. But we've exhausted the subject of college.

"Oh, I've got to meet Mike in the lunchroom," she says.

Then out of the blue she adds, "We should hang out sometime. You know, Mike and me, and you and whoever you'd like to ask."

This takes me totally by surprise. What am I supposed to say? That I don't have a girlfriend and haven't had one since Carol Stephanovich? I broke up with her at the end of my sophomore year. We were really just kissing friends. No use getting into all that now.

So I just nod and say, "Yeah, maybe."

The Big Day

After dinner I can hardly keep my eyes open, I don't bother to check my email. I try to work on my Spanish pronunciation, but all my body wants to do is sleep. So I crash early and don't wake up again until my alarm rings at 6:00 on Friday morning.

It's the big day. I'll find out this afternoon if I'm on the list of soloists. I'm a mix of fear and excitement, all at once. The rain is pounding on the roof as I head downstairs to eat breakfast.

"Raining cats and dogs," Dad says, as I walk into the kitchen. He's cooking eggs and sausage. It's a weekend breakfast on Friday.

"Big day for you. Are you excited?" he asks, as I dig into my eggs.

For some reason, I'm really hungry. I give him a half smile and nod. In the grey light of morning, I'm less certain than I was last night that I'm going to make the soloists' list. "Mostly nervous."

"When will you find out?"

"Mrs. Walker will post the names of this year's soloists on the bulletin board outside the music department office sometime around noon."

"I have a feeling you're going to make it," Dad says. "But whatever happens, I'm going to take you to that Thai place you like in the city to celebrate. And since it's raining so hard, I'll take you to school."

Knowing what a big day it is for me, I think he probably would have driven me even if it hadn't been raining. I wait nervously through my morning classes and finally walk past the music office on my way to lunch. This way, if I'm not selected, I can spend my lunch in the library, away from any choir members I might run into in the lunchroom.

There is quite a crowd looking at the bulletin board when I get there, and I have some trouble getting close enough to see the names.

"Wow," someone says. "Looks like all the seniors made it."

My heart feels like it is going to jump out of my chest.

"Robin," says a voice from behind me.

I turn around and there's Kelly. She's wearing one of her peasant dresses. It looks like the one she almost got kicked out of school for. She's smiling her big Kelly smile, and before I can say anything, her arms wrap around me in a big hug.

"Congratulations."

I stare at her, speechless.

"You haven't seen the list yet?" she asks after a moment.

"No." Now my heart is pounding.

I smile weakly at Kelly. Then I turn and push my way into the crowd that's standing in front of the bulletin board. And there it is, the list of the choir soloists for this year. At first the names are blurry. So I have to edge a little bit closer to read the names on the typed list:

<u>Male Soloists 2008-09 School Year</u>:
Dixon Archer
Alan Brooks
Phineas Kelly
Robin Steele

I'm on the list. I made it. Wow! I stand there in kind of a daze, until people start congratulating me.

"Congratulations Steele."

"Well deserved, Robin."

"I'm so happy for you Robin." It's Keira and she's smiling. Of course, she'll once again be a soprano soloist.

"Were you nervous?" she asks.

"Just a little, "I say, finally cracking a smile, finally starting to relax.

"Maybe we can sing a duet," she says as she hugs me.

Kelly steps back beside us. "How do you feel, Robin?" she asks.

"I'm finally going to solo," I say, as if I still can't quite believe it, but it's there in black and white on the bulletin board. "I'm finally going to solo."

And then, as that reality sinks in, my body explodes with excitement. I thrust my right fist into the air, and I yell out, "Woo, I made it. I'm finally going to solo."

By the end of school, I am so hyped up that I don't wait for the bus. I just take off walking. I need to burn off some energy. *I'm finally going to solo.* All the way home that's all I can think about. I can't wait to tell Dad and email Mike that I'm officially a soloist.

This has got to be the best day of my life. I want to tell the world—everybody except maybe Mom. It's stopped raining, but as I walk up the hill toward our house, I notice that the sky is strangely divided between ominous slate-grey clouds to the north and white fluffy clouds mixed with patches of sky blue to the south. It's striking and a little bit unsettling.

"OK, let's talk this over," I hear Dad say as I come in the door. He's talking with somebody on the landline in his workroom. He hears me come in and acknowledges me with a little wave as I walk by his open door. I can tell by the tone of his voice that he's having a serious conversation and that it's with Mom.

I go to the kitchen and get an apple and some milk from the refrigerator. From the kitchen table, I can clearly hear Dad's side of the conversation, but there are a lot of aggravating pauses when Mom is speaking.

"I know this is important. But . . . I know you've been dissatisfied with the pace of the investigation."

I should probably go up to my room, but instead I keep listening.

"OK, I know. But are you sure it will actually help if you stay?" He's silent for a moment. "I understand how you feel and why," he says, a sense of urgency in his voice. He's silent again, then I hear him say, "I know it's our daughter we're talking about. I'm just saying if you stay you need to stay under control . . . Just think about what I've said. Will you, please?"

Dad waits for an answer, then says. "Have you talked to Dan?" A moment passes before he says, "Good. What did he say?" This time he pauses for just a few seconds then says, "You know we can't afford to have you lose your job." His voice sounds harder now, like he's determined to make this point. "Yes, I know how you feel about that. But I'm just saying . . . Well, I'm just saying that Dan has been very understanding about letting you go back to Maine. And you don't want to alienate him by taking off more time than is absolutely necessary."

There's a long pause. I hear Mom's voice. It's louder now, but I can't make out what she's saying.

"I just want to know that he's OK with this." There's frustration in Dad's voice. Then he pauses to listen to Mom. "OK, OK. So Robin has just gotten home from school. Do you want to talk with him? You could tell him your news." Pause. He waits a moment, then says, "He's working hard and everything has been going fine."

Dad calls my name. He must have thought I was upstairs because he seems surprised when I come out of the kitchen. "Your mom wants to say hi." He's forcing a smile when he hands me the phone.

"Hi Robin," Mom says immediately.

"Hi."

"How's school going?"

What should I tell her? A few minutes ago, I was euphoric about being picked to sing solos in the choir, but I know Mom doesn't want to hear about that.

"Fine," I say finally. "The big oral report due yesterday in AP Environmental Science went pretty well."

"Good. I hope we can count on mostly A's this year," she says

I can tell from the tone of her voice that this is the kind of thing she wants to hear, not stuff about choir or soloing, or Nancy asking me to double date with her and Mike—definitely not the last. I'm hoping for mostly A's too—I need to get as many A's as possible—but Mom hasn't helped at all with all her rules and restrictions.

"So I have some big news," Mom says. "As I was just telling your dad, they found Toby's pink sun hat on the beach on an island called Isle au Haut."

A bunch of stuff goes flashing through my head— Toby running around the little island off shore from

Bill's house and then me racing around trying to find her, the look on everyone's face when they realized what had happened, and how mad Mom was with me when she found out Toby was missing. The last thing that comes into my mind is the image of Toby's floppy little pink sun hat washing up on the shore of some island, and the thought that she must be dead.

"Do you know what this means, Robin?"

"What?" I ask.

"This is our first big lead. It's quite a ways from Bill's. But now we know that Toby is still in or around the area. And if I can finally get the police up here to just do something right, I believe we'll find her."

There's a pause. I can hear her breathing on the other end of the line.

"Robin, this horrible nightmare is about to be over. We're going to find Toby. I know it. And she's going to be OK. She may be hurt. She may be scared. I don't know. But we're going to find her and take her home, and from now on we'll keep her safe."

I can hardly believe what I'm hearing.

"I'm going to have to stay here for a little while longer to see that the police follow up properly on this lead. I'll keep you guys informed, and when we find her, I'll call right away. OK?"

A chill goes up my spine. In my mind, I can see Toby's little pink sun hat lying on a beach somewhere in Penobscot Bay. And what I think that means is that Toby is probably dead. But that's not what Mom thinks. And what Mom thinks is what driving us now.

When I don't respond right away, Mom says, "You don't sound very excited."

"It's kind of a shock."

"Yes, I know you and your dad didn't believe that I could find her. But I always believed we would, and now it's only a matter of days before we do. And really, given what happened, we should be so happy, particularly you and I. Soon Toby will be back home. Isn't that wonderful?"

"Sure," I say finally.

Maybe Mom is right. I always figured that Toby's disappearance would have a dramatic ending. She would reappear to tell us that she had escaped from pirates or kidnappers, or that she had suffered temporary amnesia, only to remember who she was when she saw her picture on the news, or that she had stowed away on somebody's sailing boat going to Canada. Whatever happened to her, I knew it would make a great story because Toby is such a little drama queen.

Part 3

Maine Again

CHAPTER TWENTY

Finding Planet X

Dad says at dinner, "Your mom sounded really good over the telephone." He's trying to make it sound like everything is cool, but I can tell by the look on his face that he's worried.

I'd gone to my room while he and Mom were still talking. After he finished, he knocked on my door and said he still wanted to take me out to celebrate my being selected to solo.

Then, at dinner, we talk mostly about my day, or rather I talk, and he mostly listens. "I didn't think I'd make it," I keep saying. "There are so many good singers in the choir, I didn't think Mrs. Walker would choose me."

"But she did," Dad says. "You worked hard and sang your heart out, so she did."

"Some choir members said Mrs. Walker was just picking seniors. But Phinney Kelly and Monique Jackson aren't seniors, and they're both going to solo."

"Don't second-guess your director. You worked hard and got picked. OK? Any idea when you are going to sing?"

"No, maybe we'll find out something on Wednesday."

It feels so good to be talking to Dad about soloing, something I've wanted to do since I joined the choir, something I had tried out for as a junior. And now finally I've made it. I am going to solo. But even as I'm feeling the glow of being selected, I'm having to push one big fear out of my mind.

"I'm just afraid—"

Dad interrupts. "That you won't be good enough?"

"Yeah, sorta," I say, except it's not actually that simple. I am nervous about soloing. But what I'm most worried about, I'm not sure I want to mention to Dad. Maybe I should just wait to see what happens.

"You can surprise your mom with your news the next time she calls."

A flash of anxiety hits me. My first thought after I heard Dad talking with her on the phone was: *what's Mom going to say when she hears I tried out to solo?* "I'm afraid Mom's not going to want me to solo," I tell him.

Dad looks up from his plate of Pad Thai, and frowns. "I'll talk to her if she objects. But this antagonism between the two of you has to stop."

I immediately feel defensive, which I guess Dad can tell by the look on my face

"Look, Robin, I know your mom has been tough on you. But it's only because she expects so much of you, and because . . ." He stops in midsentence.

"You guys don't know how it is to be grounded for over a whole month. I'm seventeen. It's bad enough I don't have a cell phone. I don't have a car. And now I can't even go out on weekends with friends. That's not fair! It's just not fair."

Dad sighs and rubs his forehead. I notice how lined his forehead has become. Was it that way before Maine? He looks tired and sad.

"It's both your faults because neither of you have been willing to sit down and talk through your feelings about what happened . . . and why."

I don't say anything. Dad sighs again. He's disappointed in me too—not like Mom's disappointed, but still disappointed.

"Anyway, when she gets home, I'm going to insist that the two of you sit down and talk."

We both go back to eating. Talking about Mom ends our happy celebration. All the way home Dad is quiet. I can't tell if he is mad or just thinking. When we get home, Dad suggests we go into the kitchen.

"Let's sit down and talk," he says.

For some reason, Dad likes to sit in the kitchen when he has something he thinks is really important to talk about. He pours a glass of wine and I get water. I've had beer before. I think my parents know it, but they've never said anything. Of course, they wouldn't allow me to drink alcohol at home. But I did have a glass of wine at a party Keira had for her friends after our final choir performance last spring. It tasted acidic and gave me a headache. So, as much as I wish he considered me old enough to have a glass of wine with him, I really don't want one.

We sit down at our old wooden kitchen table and drink in silence for a few minutes. I can tell Dad's thinking about something. Finally, he clears his throat and says, "You know, when I didn't get tenure at the university, your mom was pretty angry with me."

I remember hearing them argue about his leaving UW. And I vaguely remember Mom saying something about Dad being irresponsible. But the hard feelings, which lasted for quite a while, made me nervous, so for a few months I spent a lot of time either in my room or over at Mike's.

"Yeah, I remember. Mom was pretty pissed, but I never really knew why."

"It's hard to explain and maybe even harder to admit. "I've always enjoyed teaching, but to work permanently at the university you have to get tenure, and that meant that I had to do original research. I'd been an assistant professor for three years and then was rehired for a second three-year term. But I either had to be offered tenure during that period, or I had to leave. So I was feeling some pressure, and that's why I started going over to Ellensburg to gather data at the university's Manastash Ridge Observatory. Remember, I took you over there with me once."

"Yeah, what a cool place!"

Dad smiles and I can tell he's remembering what a great time we had on that sunny September weekend trip to the observatory.

"But I couldn't really decide what I wanted to work on, so I started looking at the Kuiper Belt to see what I could find that was new and interesting. For quite a while, I had an interest in the theory that there might be a mysterious extra planet, a Planet X, that was affecting the orbits of the outer planets and other Kuiper Belt objects."

Dad doesn't have to ask if I know what the Kuiper Belt is. We talked about it that weekend we spent at the observatory. When our solar system was forming, there was a lot of material and gas, moving around. Some of this stuff coalesced into the planets, moons, and asteroids. But some of it, for various reasons, didn't, and that got knocked out to the far reaches of the solar system beyond Neptune. There it formed a belt of icy, rocky objects that are spinning around our sun. But what, I wonder, is Planet X?

"Planet X?" I ask?

"Yeah, it's an idea that goes way back. Early astronomers thought that the mass of Neptune was big enough that Uranus should have a standard orbit. But the orbit of Uranus is irregular, which led to speculation that it was being affected by another large planet. That idea became really popular in the early twentieth century when two astronomers, Percival Lowell and William Pickering, using telescope observations, predicted the location of another gas giant, which they called the ninth planet, outside the orbit of what, at the time, were the solar system's eight planets."

"When Pluto was discovered in 1930, it became the solar system's ninth planet, and speculation about another larger planet somewhere outside these first nine planets stopped, at least for a while. But then Pluto turned out to be too small and its orbit too elliptical to be a good candidate for a Planet X."

"Poor Pluto. First, it's not big enough to be considered Planet X, and now it's no longer even considered to be a planet."

Dad smiles. He doesn't smile a lot, but he's got a nice smile when he does. Apparently, it was his smile that first attracted Mom. When I was a kid and he was working at UW, he always seemed pretty happy, and I remember him smiling and laughing when we were together. Mom did too. All that changed after Dad lost his job.

"You know, I was one of a minority of astronomers who believed that Pluto should not have been demoted to dwarf planet status. But it's certainly not a Planet X. Anyway, over time the search for a fifth large gas giant started up again, and many astronomers spent a lot time trying to either find it or come up with some other explanation for the orbital irregularities of objects at the edge of the solar system, particularly Uranus. But then in 1989, the Voyager spacecraft flew by Neptune and sent back data that undercut the reasoning behind the Planet X theory. Neptune's mass was less than originally thought, and when this new data was used in a simulation, it accounted for the irregularities in the Uranus orbit. The evidence suggesting a Planet X seemed to be gone."

"You mean there's no Planet X?" I ask.

"Well, that's the current opinion of the astronomical community."

"But you didn't agree?"

"I thought we'd jumped to that conclusion too early. We already knew there were other big Kuiper Belt objects, objects just smaller than Pluto, and when I was doing my observations, I started to notice that certain of these objects were lined up in such a way that it looked like some larger object was affecting their orbits. So I had a couple graduate students check my observations, and they seemed to be correct."

"And were they?"

"I thought so, and that meant I had found the area of research that might get me tenure. So I gathered data and did more calculations on and off for almost a year. Then, using our data, a graduate student and I determined that a gigantic planet about twenty-five times further from the Sun than the orbit of Neptune could have the kind of impact on Kuiper Belt objects that we had observed. We even thought we'd pinpointed where the planet might be."

"Wow."

"Yeah, except that when I drafted an article based on our findings and gave it to a senior professor in the department to review and comment on, he gave me a list of problems with the data and, as he presumed, with the conclusions. He also mentioned a couple of other areas where he thought I could get grant money to another research project, but he warned me that I was running out of time to make a change."

"So what did you do?"

"We went back and looked at all the data again. One or two of our calculations were a little off. I didn't really think that changed our observations enough to weaken the conclusions. But we corrected them, and then I had another faculty member review our material. His only comment was that he thought I should strengthen my supporting material. But he didn't criticize the basic thrust of the article.

"So, feeling OK about our data, and with only four weeks until my tenure committee was supposed to meet, I submitted the article to a major journal for publication."

"And?"

"They rejected it."

"Wow! Why?"

"It's complicated. The main reason they gave was that my conclusions were not completely supported by the data. When I asked the Dean if he could intercede, he suggested that I pick another area of research where I could get grant funding. He said he would then intercede and ask that I be given more time to gather data and write a new article.

"But I had effectively run out of time. It takes a minimum of a year to get an article published in an official journal. My tenure committee would have accepted as evidence of publication a letter from a recognized astronomy journal promising to publish my article in a particular issue. But I didn't have that."

"You couldn't do something else?"

Dad frowns and then shrugs. "Well, I was exhausted and really stressed. I thought that starting another research project from scratch would have meant cutting my classes way back—maybe teaching only one day a week—and spending the rest of my time gathering data and writing. Well, we couldn't have lived on such a limited salary, and besides, I really loved teaching my classes. But when I talked with your mom about it, she just said, 'Do it. Ditch your classes or take unpaid leave if you have to, but do it.'"

"That's just like Mom. She can be so hard."

"So anyway, she got pretty angry when I didn't. She accused me of being irresponsible. She said that I liked to spend my time talking about 'big ideas and new discoveries,' rather than doing the kind of hard work that leads to them."

Even as Dad is talking, I find myself thinking that maybe Mom was right. Because if Dad had gotten tenure and stayed at UW, everything else would have been different.

Dad shrugs. "Looking back, she may have had a point." I can tell he is struggling with the memory of what happened.

"But I was angry too."

"At Mom?"

"Well, sort of, though mostly at the department and at myself. Neither the dean nor the head of the tenure committee seemed excited about the idea of more research on a hypothetical Planet X. Research is big deal at the university, and getting grant money to fund projects is also a big deal. I think they wanted me to do something that was more 'practical' and more likely to pick up a grant."

"By then I was pretty tired. When I met with my tenure committee, I asked the committee to give me a six-month extension to try to gather more data and to rewrite the article. But they weren't really much help. They finally gave me three months. They said that if I changed my area of research, they would consider giving me more time. But for some reason, that offer just made me angry.

"Your mom wanted me to try something, either revising my original article or changing my subject. But, even if I had gotten more time, completing something so complex with so little time, seemed impossible, or at least I convinced myself that it was impossible, so I just gave up."

Dad looks so sad. I guess he's wondering if I'll be mad at him, too, just like Mom was, now that I know what happened.

"Anyway, your mom and I eventually talked things out and agreed to look forward, not backward, and to try to forgive and forget. Maybe I wasn't meant to be college professor. I don't know. But things were pretty tough for us for a while."

I feel sad for Dad now that I know what happened, and I'm thinking as I hear him talk that if anyone should understand how hard it is for me to talk with Mom, it would be him.

"I don't think Mom cares how I feel," I say.

"Well, Robin, I think she needs to hear how you feel because you haven't really talked about that. And I think you need to hear how she feels and why. That's the only way you two can start to repair your relationship."

Maybe Dad's expecting a response, but I don't say anything.

"If you do this now," he says after a moment, "it would be the best for both of you."

Well, that might be what Dad thinks, and that might be what he and Mom had to do after the tenure fiasco. But what I know is that I don't want to talk with Mom about Toby, at least not until we know what has actually happened.

"OK," I say finally. But I don't really mean it. Anyway, it doesn't matter what I say. I know this sharing of feelings thing isn't going to happen because Mom's not interested either.

Chapter Twenty-One

Message from Maude

After breakfast on Saturday morning, we get to work on my early action applications for Western and UW. Now it's almost noon, and I'm getting tired.

"Can we take a break? I'd like to check my email."

"Sure," Dad says, "but we're almost through with the application to Western. Let's finish it now and then start the one for UW after lunch. And could you limit your email time to a half hour and then come down and help me make lunch?"

I'm expecting, actually hoping, to get a message from Mike. But when I open my email, I get a big surprise. The first email in my new mailbox is from Maude:

Hi Robin,

I was hoping to surprise you with a text, but Bill said you don't text, so he gave me your email address. I guess you had lost mine? He also said that your sister was still missing, and thought you'd like to hear from a friend. I hope you're OK.

My big news is that I've been tentatively accepted at RISD, and I'm in the running to get an internship in Providence for part of next summer. I still have to go to Providence the weekend after next to do a graded art project and be interviewed by a committee. But I'm feeling pretty confident and really, really excited. I'm so ready to be away from Belfast.

How is your senior year going? Given what's going on with your sister, I hope you've been able to stay focused.? That's so important in your senior year. For me, the motivation to not just ditch another year at Belfast High has been RISD and a brand-new life on the horizon. Have you done any early action applications? Which schools did you decide to apply to? Don't get discouraged if you don't get into Berkeley.

Listen to me: so many questions.

Anyway, how's choir? I was impressed when you told me you were a singer. I play the violin. But my voice is gross.

We've had some great September weather. I hang out and draw by the bay every chance I get, and sometimes I think about when you and I walked the beach and talked about our lives. I've seen the osprey flying around—you know, the one we saw circling the little island that day. It likes to sit in the big elm tree north of Bill's house, and sometimes it swoops down over the island and then heads east out over the bay.

So it's your turn now. What's up with you? Here's my cell number 207-585-5229, in case you want to call sometime, or you can always email.

—Maude

I go back and read Maude's email two more times. It's not enough. I wish she'd written more, and I want to write her back right now and tell her everything, answer all her questions, and especially tell her about being picked to solo. I think about calling her. Mom would never let me, but maybe Dad would be OK with it. For now, maybe I should just email.

Dad's calling from the bottom of the stairs: "Robin, I need your help with lunch. Finish up whatever you're doing."

Shit! I can't do anything now. I need time to think about what I should say. I start to shut down my computer and then I notice an email from Mike:

Robbie Hood,

Congrats on getting picked to solo with the choir. I haven't had much free time, but now that you've met Nancy, maybe the three of us could get together for a movie or something. Nancy thinks we should double date, but the last I heard you didn't have a steady honey, or even an occasional squeeze. Maybe you could ask Kelly?

Anyway, it's something to think about!! See you in class.

—Mike

How weird. First, I get an email from the one girl in the world I could really be interested in—who incidentally lives in Maine. And then I get an email from Mike asking me to double date with him and Nancy.

Dad and I finish my early action application for UW after lunch. Getting Maude's email has filled me with energy. Maybe that's a good sign. It would be so great if I could somehow stay connected with Maude. But by dinner time, I start to wonder if the good stuff that happened today will change anything with Mom coming home and Toby still missing.

Chapter Twenty-Two

Affairs of the Heart

I get up early the next morning. I want to start an email to Maude after breakfast. Dad is watching one those Sunday morning political talk shows. Two guys are talking about the election and the second presidential debate, which is about a week away. One says that Obama has such a wide lead in the big states, with lots of electoral votes that the Republican candidate will have to do especially well in the second debate to have a chance of winning. The other counters that the Republicans are within "striking distance" in enough of the swing states to win.

"So the race for the presidency will continue," says the interviewer as the program ends.

Dad gets up from his chair when he hears me going into the kitchen. "All they're interested in is the horserace, never the issues or the candidate's ideas," he says as he follows me into the kitchen

"What?" I ask. Politics is the last thing I have on my mind this morning.

"The media," Dad says. "All they talk about are the polls and who is ahead of whom in this state or that state. We're still struggling to get out of a recession, but you'd think from listening to the television talk shows that the election was just a horserace with nothing more at stake than a blue ribbon."

Dad doesn't usually let these things bother him, especially things on television. In fact, he seldom watches TV, and our, Toby's and my, television watching is limited to a couple hours on weekends. But this morning Dad is looking and acting tired.

"Get some breakfast, Robin. I want to go to the 11:00 service at the UU church."

Mom and Dad call themselves agnostics. That doesn't mean nonbelievers. It means they're not sure what they believe. But that's a little confusing, too, because I know they both believe in certain things. Mom likes to talk about a life force in nature and in people, and Dad believes that there are truths about life that are slowly being revealed to us through science.

Dad says he grew up "unchurched." I guess that means his family never set foot in a church. Mom, of course, was the daughter of a Unitarian minister. We seldom go to church, but when we do, we go to the Unitarian church in North City.

I get cereal and make some toast. I want to ask Dad if I can just stay at home, but I can tell he is anxious to go, and when I try to bring it up, he knows what I'm going to say before I do.

"I want us both to go," is all he says. I decide not to argue. I can wait until we get back to email Maude.

You can easily pick out the Unitarian church from the Presbyterian church one block to the north, and the Methodist church one block to the south in North City. The Unitarian church is long and low with lots of windows and a couple skylights. It has no cross or steeple or stained glass windows. The building is lighter inside and has a wood-walled sanctuary. The only similarity with the other two churches is that the Unitarians do have an organ.

The minister's sermon turns out to be about forgiveness. Dad listens intently. I can tell he's taking in every word, but it just makes me feel uncomfortable. On the way out of the sanctuary, a couple of people nod to Dad or say hello. One woman tries to talk with him, but he just brushes past her as he pushes me toward the door.

There's a line of people, just outside the sanctuary, waiting to shake the minister's hand, or make some comment about the sermon. Dad steers us past the crowd and toward the door, when someone calls out his name. It's the minister, Mr. Low, a husky man with grey hair. He's stepped away from the line of folks waiting to talk with him and is walking toward us.

"Mr. Steele, it's nice to see you," Mr. Low says, a concerned look on his face.

Dad nods in acknowledgment. I wonder if Mr. Low knows about Toby. After all we haven't been to church since we got back from Maine.

"Hello, Robin," he says to me. Then he turns back to Dad and adds, "I was really sorry to hear about your daughter."

Dad stops. He looks uncomfortable, like he doesn't know what to say, or maybe he just can't bring himself to say anything.

"Someone from our Care Committee talked to your wife last month."

Dad looks surprised when the minister mentions this.

"So, how are you holding up?"

"We're OK," Dad says. Dad doesn't want to talk about Toby, or about how it's affecting our family.

The minister looks over at me. "And how are you doing, Robin?"

Now I feel uncomfortable again, just like I was during his sermon. What am I supposed to say? That Mom hates me because of what happened. That it might ruin my final year at West High. That Toby's disappearance may have been my fault. I don't think so.

"OK, I guess," I say unconvincingly.

"Toby is such a happy and talkative young lady. I'll keep her and you both in my thoughts, and we'll hope for the best," Mr. Low says. "But, in the meantime, if you need to talk to anyone, please call the office, and they'll be happy to make an appointment with me, or with someone from the Care Committee."

"Thanks," Dad says quietly. For the first time since the day Toby went missing, Dad looks miserable. Then he turns, and I follow him out the front door.

Was Toby happy and talkative? Or was she just irritating and pushy? I'm so confused.

We go back to the car. Then we sit there for what seems like forever while Dad stares out the window. Other people start to pass by going to their own cars. Some look at us just sitting there in the church parking lot. A couple of them pause, as though they are thinking about coming over to see if we're OK. Finally, Dad notices them.

He starts the car, sighs, looks out the window again, and then says, "Nobody can understand how terrible it is to lose a child."

By the time we get home, all I want to do is to email Maude. But Dad wants me to help him make lunch.

We don't talk much as we get things together. Dad seems preoccupied. So finally I tell him that I got an email from Maude.

"Oh, that's good," he says.

He leafs through the Sunday *New York Times* as we're eating lunch. But he doesn't stop to read any of the articles.

After lunch, I head for the computer and spend about an hour working on an email to Maude. At first, I try to sound totally upbeat, but that feels really bogus. So then I try talking about how I'm feeling about things, but that sounds way too whiney. Then I look at what Maude wrote—no melodrama just facts—and I try doing that same thing.

Hi Maude,

Congratulations about getting accepted to RISD. I can tell you're really excited. I'm sure you'll make a great impression on the selection committee. My big news is that I auditioned and got selected to solo this year with the choir. I'm not sure exactly when or what I'll be singing. But I'm pretty excited too.

Yes, things were a little tense after we got back home. Mom was pretty upset about Toby and kind of took it out on me. But I stayed focused on school and choir, and once Mom left for Maine, and with Dad now at home, things have gotten almost back to normal. Of course, we're all still hoping the police will find Toby.

You said that you were impressed when I told you I was a singer. Wow! I think it's amazing that someone like you who's an honor student, president of the art and math clubs, and an artist who also plays the violin is impressed by someone like me who sings in a school choir.

Dad helped me fill out the early action applications for the University and Western yesterday. That's why I didn't get around to answering your email until today. I'll mail them off tomorrow. I don't know yet what I'm going to do about Berkeley.

Anyway, it was great to hear from you. And thanks for giving me your cell phone number. Email is the safest way to talk right now. Feel free to email whenever you want.

—Robin

Pretty bold, huh?

I spend another hour thinking about what I'd said, and what I should have said, changing it, and then end up sending the original message. After dinner, I check my email again to see if I've gotten a response. There's nothing from Maude. But there is new mail. It's from Kelly.

Hi Robin,

Surprise! Mike gave me your email address. I hope that's OK. Nancy and I were talking, and she brought up the idea of the four of us doing something together. So anyway, I suggested that maybe the three of you could come to the opening night performance of the *Three Penny Opera* and that after the play we could go out somewhere in the District.

Does this sound like fun? I think it would be fun. Mike said you don't text. So, think about it and let me know what you think, and I hope you're OK with this email. And I hope that things are going better for you, too, and that you'll be able to come to the play.

—Kelly

Chapter Twenty-Three

Questions

I guess I've known for a while that Kelly is interested in me. And hey, why not! I'm a pretty cool guy. In a strange way, Kelly and Maude are a lot alike. They are both artists. Maude draws, paints, writes poetry, and plays the violin. Kelly acts and sings. But that's where the comparison ends.

Kelly makes it a point to talk with me whenever she gets a chance, which is mostly at choir practice. She's nice enough, but I've never thought about asking her out. I don't think of her that way, and lately her chattering has been a little irritating.

It would be fun to double date with Mike and Nancy, although Kelly wouldn't be the girl I'd want to go with. She's just a choir friend. But none of that matters because my parents, especially Mom, would never let me go—not now. I could ask Dad, but why would I? I know what the answer would be.

Monday morning, when I come downstairs for breakfast, Dad looks even more tired than he did on Sunday. He says he was up early talking with Mom. She's flying home Wednesday night.

I see Mike in a couple of classes on Monday. We say hi, but when he asks about double dating, I tell him that Mom is coming home on Wednesday and that I'd have to clear it with her. He seems surprised.

"That sucks. I thought all that house arrest stuff would have ended by now."

"Well, Dad's a little more lenient than Mom, but when she gets home, I'll have to talk with them both—especially Mom—about anything I want to do."

"No chance, huh?"

I shrug my shoulders. To me the answer is obvious.

"You ought to talk to the ACLU about suing your parents for false imprisonment or something," Mike says.

"Yeah, great idea."

Mike smiles, like he's thinking this is really funny, and that it might even be possible. But it isn't funny, and it certainly isn't going to happen.

On Tuesday morning, I hear Dad talking on the phone when I crawl out of bed. As I walk into the kitchen, Dad is sitting there drinking his coffee and staring out the window.

"Good morning Robin," he says without his usual smile.

Then before I can say anything, he adds, "I talked with your Mom a few minutes ago. She's a little upset. I'm not completely sure why, but she's flying back on Wednesday afternoon. I'll pick you up right after school, and we'll drive to the airport."

Wow, that's really not what I needed to hear.

As I leave Mrs. Gardner's class before lunch, Nancy stops me just outside the door. "Robin, Kelly says she emailed you about the four of us getting together to see her play on Friday, and hang out afterwards. So can you come? It should be fun."

Nancy must be the one pushing this idea. I can just imagine what she's thinking. Mike probably told her I'm this lonely guy who doesn't have a regular girlfriend, and she's decided that Kelly and I would be the perfect match. But I'm starting to find this a little annoying.

"I'm not sure if I can."

"Why? Kelly is nice, and I know she likes you."

"Yeah, I know Kelly. We're both in choir, but I'm sort of on probation because of something that happened this summer."

"I heard your little sister went missing, but what has that got to do with you?"

"Look," I say not wanting to get into a discussion about Toby with Nancy. "Look, it's complicated, but right now, I'm only able to do activities that are connected with school, like choir."

Nancy frowns. "So, what's her name?" she asks.

"Toby."

"How old is she?"

"Eight. She's eight," I say, trying to sound as annoyed as possible.

"So what happened?"

"Nothing," I say. Now I'm really getting irritated. If Nancy asks me any more questions, I'm going to tell her it's none of her business.

Just then Mike comes out of the AP classroom. He puts his arm around Nancy's shoulder. "Hey Robbie, have you talked to Kelly? Are we double dating on Friday?" he asks.

"No."

"Why?" Nancy asks.

"My mother is coming back from Maine on Wednesday night. She's likely to be tired, so it's not a good idea for me to bring up doing anything social until she's been home for at least a day."

"Why do you have to ask permission to go out on a Friday night?"

I feel like just breaking off this conversation. "I just do," I say, unable to hide the irritation in my voice.

Nancy gives me a look that tells me she could never understand my situation. Then Mike jumps in and says, "You should at least email Kelly to let her know why you can't go."

Suddenly, things have become very awkward.

"OK, it's lunchtime," Mike says, steering Nancy away from me and toward the lunchroom. "Email me," he says as he turns to go.

I watch them melt into the crowd of students who are headed either to lunch or to class.

On Wednesday, I wait till the last minute to show up for choir. Kelly is already on the riser in the alto section. When she smiles at me, I put on my best 'I'm late for choir' act and ignore her.

Mrs. Walker says she wants to speak with the soloists after rehearsal. When rehearsal ends, I notice Kelly heading my way. I knew this would happen because I need to stay in the auditorium until I talk with Mrs. Walker. But I'm hoping that Kelly will just leave after I tell her I don't think this double-dating thing is a going to work out.

"Hi, Robin," she says.

"Hi, Kelly."

"Could we talk?"

"Sure, but I've only got until Mrs. Walker calls me."

"If I wait around, can we talk after you're through?"

"Can't," I say. "Dad's picking me up to go to the airport with him to pick up my mom."

"Oh, did you get my email about the play?"

I nod. "But I doubt my parents will agree. I'm still kind of on probation."

"That's too bad. You guys were going to be my invitees to opening night. It's really a great play."

The expression on her face tells me this is important to her.

"I just thought it would be fun," she says with a sigh. But her face is saying, "Please come," and I'm starting to feel bad.

"Yeah, look I'll check with my parents tomorrow. But it's really out of my hands."

Kelly smiles tentatively. "Do you think there's any chance they'll let you go?"

"Honestly, I doubt it," but then I add, "Who knows? Dad might say yes, but Mom will be a tough sell."

"That's too bad. It must be very painful for her, but it seems kind of harsh. What actually happened in Maine?"

There's that question again? The one I don't want to answer in any detail. I pause for a minute. I haven't really thought much about how Mom feels about Toby's disappearance. Maybe that's what Bill and Dad meant when they said Mom and I should talk about our feelings.

"Yeah, she's been a little crazy."

Kelly looks at me, and I can tell she doesn't know what to say. And I don't know what else to say either. Then I luck out. Mrs. Walker calls my name.

"Kelly, I've got to go."

Kelly looks toward Mrs. Walker, who's standing by the piano and then back to me.

"So, you will ask your parents?"

"Yes, on Thursday," I say, mostly so that I can get away from her. But then I realize I'll have to do it.

I force a smile as I turn to leave, and Kelly adds, "Please send me an email on Thursday, once you talked with your parents. And, Robin, I'm really hoping you can come." I nod yes as I leave to talk with Mrs. Walker.

CHAPTER TWENTY-FOUR

Toby's Room

Mrs. Walker and I talk for about ten minutes. She wants me to try practicing some voice exercises to expand my range, and she gives me some sheet music for a song, "Sure on this Shining Night." She says the lyrics come from a poem.

"I am penciling you in to sing in our March concert, and you'll probably be doing a duet with one of the girls," she says. "That's a little bit in the future, but this will give you plenty of time to practice and get your voice in shape."

I'm disappointed. I wanted to solo for Christmas, but she's probably right. I need the time to prepare, and singing a duet sounds really exciting.

"You've got a good tenor voice, but you need to expand your range a little. Sometimes you sound a little scratchy. That can happen to anyone, but you need to take care of your voice. Try to cut down on the nasal congestion by using a nasal spray or something else in the morning, and an hour or so before you sing."

She hands me a flash drive. "This has some exercises I'd like you to practice. Any questions?"

I shake my head. "I'm really excited to be picked to solo," I say.

She smiles. "I think you'll do fine, Robin. Just remember, you'll have about twice as much to do to prepare for that March concert as a choir member who isn't a soloist. I expect you to be at every practice after the first of the year. And you'll need to be prepared to sing your solo in at least one of our rehearsals before the concert. So if you're having problems or need help, I expect you to let me know."

"Also, at next week's rehearsal I'll be talking a little about what my criteria were for picking soloists, and I'll also distribute copies of my 'Tips for Soloists' handout."

"And remember you'll be representing the choir when you sing. You need to take good care of yourself and your voice, so you can give a good performance."

Dad is waiting for me when I leave the auditorium.

"Ready to see your mom?" He is trying to sound relaxed and excited, but I can tell he's nervous.

I shrug and fasten my seat belt.

"How was practice?" Dad asks as we drive away from school.

"Good. I got my solo assignment. But I won't be singing until the spring concert in March."

"Well, that should give you plenty of time to practice. What's your song, or do you know that yet?"

"It's something called 'Sure on this Shining Night.'"

"Oh, yeah, 'Sure on this shining night, I weep for wonder wand'ring far alone.'"

"You know the piece?"

"No, but I know the poem."

I pull the sheet music out of my backpack. "It says that the words are by someone called James Agee. He was a poet?"

"He was one of those guys who did everything. He was a journalist, a novelist, and a poet."

"But it says the composer is Morten Lauridsen."

"Well, that explains it," Dad says.

"Explains what?" I ask.

"Agee wasn't a songwriter, and that poem was written back in the 1930s. So Lauridsen must have set it to music quite a bit after that."

Dad brakes to keep us from rear-ending a car that stops unexpectedly as it is getting onto the on-ramp to the freeway.

"Maybe over the weekend I can take a look at your sheet music."

Now the traffic is getting really congested. As we snake along in stop-and-go traffic, Dad changes the subject.

"Your mom's going to be really tired when she gets in. So I'm hoping we don't get into any heated discussions tonight. Remember, keep it light, Robin. Let her do most of the talking, and don't respond if she says anything that upsets you. She's been under a lot of strain. Don't say anything about your soloing right away. There will be time to talk about that tomorrow or over the weekend. OK?"

"Yeah." I'm dreading this.

It takes us over an hour to get to the airport. But Mom's plane doesn't get in until 5:45, so we make it easily to the security gates and are waiting when we see her walking up the ramp toward us. For a moment I hardly recognize her. Her hair looks like it hasn't been combed, and her blouse and pants are mismatched, like she put them on without really thinking. As she gets closer, I notice the dark circles under her eyes and how drawn and tired she looks.

She smiles weakly as she comes through security, and nobody says much until we get into the car. On the way home, Dad tries to make small talk. I just keep quiet. All Mom says is that she hasn't been sleeping very well, but that she was able to sleep a bit on the plane.

Dad's tuna noodle isn't too bad, and he prepared some fresh asparagus to go along with the casserole. At dinner, Mom just picks at her food, eating little bits, but mostly drinking coffee.

"They haven't really made any headway at all in finding Toby," she says finally.

I follow Dad's advice and just listen. For now he can ask the questions.

"So finding Toby's sunhat hasn't helped?" Dad asks.

"According to the sheriff, all that proves is that Toby was in the water and lost her hat."

"So when they found the hat, did they search the island?"

"Apparently, Isle au Haut is part of the national park, so it was a day visitor who found the hat on the beach. That person took it to a park ranger, and by the time the ranger contacted the sheriff, the person who had found the hat was gone. The sheriff said that the rangers weren't even sure where the hat was found. Can you believe it?"

Drinking coffee and talking about the search for Toby is making Mom agitated.

"That's discouraging," says Dad. "No other leads? No one's come forward with information?"

"Apparently there were a couple of local sightings of a girl that someone thought might be Toby. But again, according to the sheriff, they amounted to nothing. Still it took the state police almost three days to put out an Amber Alert on Toby. Unbelievable, totally unbelievable!"

Now Mom's really getting worked up now.

"Anyway, they're completely incompetent when it comes to this sort of thing. If a missing child isn't found in a few days, they quickly run out of ideas. They depend totally on someone from the public telling them where to look."

"What do they think are the chances of finding Toby?" asks Dad.

"They're not saying anything specific, just that the search is continuing. But I can tell you from talking to both the sheriff and state police that the longer they search without a result, the more likely it is they won't find her. Our best bet of finding Toby is probably through the Amber Alert."

Dad reaches over the table and touches Mom's hand. For a moment I think she's going to start crying. She sighs but then her face hardens, and she gets that determined look I've seen so many times in the past.

"So that's why I think I need to go back there and search Isle au Haut myself."

Dad eyes widen and he winces. "Can we talk about this when you've had some rest?"

Mom pulls her hand away from his, stares at him for a minute, and then goes back to nibbling on her asparagus.

After dinner, she goes upstairs, and Dad and I do the dishes. I ask him about what Mom said about returning to Maine, but all he'll say is, "We'll talk tomorrow." That's fine with me, except that I'm starting to feel that Mom's about to explode. Anyway, I go to the computer and look up my AP assignment for Thursday. It's reading. That's easy. I go up to my room to do just that, read.

I check my email about 9:00 p.m., and then read two chapters ahead in my advanced geology text. Mom's old deadline for my being in bed was 10:00.

But things have gotten a bit looser since Dad has been in charge. So it's about 10:30 when I put my textbook down and leave my room to head for the bathroom. The bathroom door is shut and I assume someone is using it. Then, on the way back to my room, I notice that the door to Toby's room is slightly ajar. I push it open and look inside. There's no one there. The room is dark and quiet, and I feel compelled to step inside.

I haven't been in Toby's room since she disappeared. Moon Pie is lying on the bed. I wonder if she comes here regularly. She lifts her head and looks at me, and then lies back down and closes her eyes.

The room is full of Toby: her clothes, her posters, the little radio/CD player that our parents gave her last Christmas, and her photos, lots and lots of photos. There are photos of Moon Pie, of her friends Millie and Sable, some of Mom and Dad, including the scandalous photo of Mom in her underwear, assorted pictures of things like the red fire hydrant across the street and the old rundown barn at the end of the block, one of some deer (a doe and two fawns) eating our neighbors' roses, and a couple of me.

One in particular catches my eye. It's of Toby and me standing in the lobby of the Burke Museum. The picture was taken at Dinosaur Day a year and a half ago. Although there has never been a dinosaur skeleton found in Washington, the Burke has a decent collection of dinosaur and prehistoric mammal fossils.

After I started working at the Burke when I was fifteen, Toby began pestering me to take her to see "Robin's dinosaurs," which is what she called the dinosaurs at the Burke. So Dad dropped us off at the museum that Saturday, and we spent the morning looking through the exhibit of dinosaur replicas and fossils.

Then Toby participated in a *Drawing a Dinosaur* activity for kids.

In the picture, I'm holding her left hand, and she's holding up her drawing of an Allosaurus with her right hand. Toby was so proud of that drawing. Across the bottom, she had written: "My big brother Robin and me at the museum." I had forgotten about that afternoon and how much fun we had. Toby seemed excited about everything that day, whether it was learning about a new dinosaur or prehistoric mammal, or talking to the paleontologists who were displaying the fossils.

And she was so proud of her drawing. Toby and a boy had a contest during the dinosaur drawing activity to see who could draw the best Allosaurus. When both had finished their drawings, they declared the contest a tie, and everybody—Toby, the boy, his mother and me—laughed. Then she asked one of the museum workers to take a picture of us while she held up her drawing. As I look at the photo of her drawing, I feel a wave of sadness wash over me. *Oh, Moon Pie, where is she*?

The cat looks and me and then jumps off the bed.

"Shouldn't you be in bed?"

I turn and there's Mom standing at the door. Her face is blank. I can't tell if she's angry or just exhausted.

"I guess. I lost track of time reading for geology. And then I noticed that this door was open on my way to the bathroom."

She's looking at Toby's photo of us at the Burke. When she holds out her hand and I give it to her, she sighs. After a moment, she hands it back and says, "Put it away and get to bed."

I can tell she doesn't want an argument. I put the picture back with the others on Toby's dresser and walk past Mom and out of the room. A couple of minutes later, on my way back from the bathroom, I notice that Toby's door is closed. I wonder if Mom is still in there, or if she has gone to bed.

Mom is downstairs when I go down for breakfast Thursday morning. She and Dad are talking when I walk into the kitchen. Both sound angry, but I can't tell why. They stop talking as soon as they see me. Dad goes back to reading his paper and Mom to drinking her coffee. By the time I sit down to eat my cereal, Mom has gone back upstairs.

Going back to school on Thursday is a relief, and nothing eventful happens until I get to geology lab at the end of the day. But while we're working in lab, Mike asks me about going to the play on Friday. I tell him the same thing I told Kelly yesterday. But I add that it's probably a waste of time for me to ask my parents if I can go to something on Friday night because Mom is sure to veto the idea.

"You can't just get an OK from your Dad?" Mike asks.

"No," I say. "If I start to go out tomorrow night and I haven't talked with Mom about it, she won't be happy and she'll stop me right away."

"I don't understand why your dad can't just talk with her about it."

Maybe he could if things were different.

"Look, Dad's walking on pins and needles since Mom got back. She wants to go back to Maine again to look for Toby."

"Wow. That's crazy," Mike says. "What about her job?"

"Don't ask me. But it was the first thing she brought up when she got home last night. I know Dad's worried, and I expect they'll be hashing it out this weekend. Anyway, I don't think he's going to want to talk to her about letting me go out on Friday night."

"That's too bad. I thought doubling with you and Kelly would be fun. Kelly's really excited about the play, and I know she really wants you to come. And dude, where would you rather be on Friday night? Home with your Mom, or out with friends?"

Mike's right. Given my situation at home, the double date idea is sounding better and better.

"Yeah, I know. I have to admit that I wasn't too excited about this double date idea when Nancy brought it up. But now that it's so close, I want to go." I pause before adding, "I'll bring it up at dinner, and then I'll email Kelly. But I'm not optimistic."

When I get home, it is clear things have gotten even worse. Mom is talking on the telephone. Dad is standing in the kitchen drinking coffee and staring out our kitchen window.

"What's going on?" I ask.

"Your mom's on the telephone with Dan."

Then, despite feeling that I shouldn't, I bring up the double date idea just to see how he reacts. "Oh," I say. "So anyway, I have something I need to ask you."

When Dad turns and looks at me, I notice that the worry lines on his forehead have gotten bigger in the last couple days.

"Mike has asked me to go with him and his girlfriend to the play at school tomorrow night. It's called the *Three Penny Opera*."

Dad frowns. "Why didn't you ask me about this earlier?"

"I didn't know until this week, and I thought with Mom coming home maybe I should wait. But Mike was asking me about it again today. He's got tickets from somebody in the play, and he wants to know if I can come."

"*Three Penny Opera*: I remember seeing that in college. So this is just to see a play at school?"

"Well, we'd probably be going out afterward for coffee or something."

"And it would just be the three of you?"

"Ah . . . the person who gave Mike the tickets will probably join us after the play. Her name's Kelly and I know her from choir."

"So this is a date?"

"Not really. It's just a few friends getting together after a play."

Dad gives me a thin smile. "I see. Well, it sounds like a date to me."

"Take my word for it. It's not a date," I say. But even as I try to reassure him, I realize how ridiculous that sounds.

There's a pause, and then Dad says, "Robin, I wish you'd talked to me about this earlier. I could have thought a little about how we could bring it up to your mom."

"Yeah, well, I wasn't even sure I was interested in going until Mike asked me about it again today."

Dad shrugs. "Maybe we can talk about it at dinner."

Just then Mom comes into the kitchen, and we both go silent.

"Cheer up," she says, forcing a smile. "I've got some good news. Dan's agreed to give me an unpaid leave of absence starting on Wednesday to go back to Maine. I've agreed to work tomorrow, Saturday, and Monday to get all my paperwork up to date, and try to finish one sale."

"Are you sure this is the right thing to do?" Dad asks. "You're looking awfully tired."

"I need to be back there to find Toby," Mom says, "and I'd like you both to come with me."

Dad puts his hands on his head like he's just gotten a bad headache. "Let's talk about this at dinner, Claire."

Mom's face turns grey, but she doesn't say anything.

I know I should leave, so I go up to my room. The first thing that comes into my mind is that if we go back to Maine, maybe I can see Maude. But then I think, what about school and what about choir? One thing is for sure, there's no way we can bring up the double-date idea now. Once Dad and Mom start arguing about whether we should go back to Maine, any chance that Mom might be willing to agree to my going on a date tomorrow night will be dead.

Before Dad lost his job at the university, I almost never heard Mom and Dad arguing, and they never used to argue in front of us kids. But since Mom went back to work, things have changed. They argue more now, and it's gotten worse since Toby disappeared. And I know that sometimes lately they are arguing about me.

We've hardly sat down for dinner, before Dad asks Mom why she thinks we need to go back to Maine. He's obviously upset with the idea.

"I just don't understand why you think we need to go back to Maine right now. I mean, you've just been there. Why not wait until we get some new information from the state police?"

"Jim, you don't understand. The state police, the sheriff, they're not going to find Toby. You're right. I've just been there, and I've seen them and talked with them. So I know they're never going to find her. They're not capable of finding Toby."

"But, Claire, how do you know that?" Dad says. "They've got the experts and resources—things like

the Amber Alert system and state police crime lab—
that we'll never have."

"I just know. I realized it after I went up to Augusta
to talk to the state police about the investigation. Bill
drove up with me. I spoke to a captain who told me
about everything they were doing, and after I left on
the drive back to Bill's, I realized that these people
were never going to find Toby."

Dad looks really frustrated. "I know you're upset
with how things are going," he says. "But if we go back
there now, we'll just be wandering around and getting
in the way."

"They will never find Toby, Jim! I know it! They will
never find her because they don't care enough. They
don't love her like we do. I realized on the flight back
that we three are the only people who can find Toby
because we're the people who love her. But it's got to
be the three of us. And Jim, we are running out of time.
I know Toby's out there somewhere alive, but we're
running out of time to find her."

After dinner, I immediately head for my laptop. The
double-date idea is dead. I can't even bring it up now
because, with Mom dead set on us all going back to
Maine, bringing up something else, particularly something social, is just a very bad idea. And there's one
thing I'm sure of after I hear Mom talk about us going
back to Maine: I know we're going. Not matter how
crazy the idea is. No matter what Dad thinks. I know
we're going.

CHAPTER TWENTY-FIVE

Back to Maine

Hi Kelly,

I'm not going to be able to go to the play tomorrow. Mom's back and there's a good chance we will all be going back to Maine next week. I'm not sure what this means or how long we'll be gone. But it can't be too long because I can't miss too much school or choir practice. Anyway, there just hasn't been a chance to bring up going out with you guys tomorrow night. So break a leg and good luck with your opening night. The double date idea did sound like fun, but it's not going to happen this time.

—Robin

I think about saying more, like telling her I talked to Dad, but he wanted me to speak directly with Mom. Then I realize that saying more won't change anything and might just lead to more questions, and I really don't want to get into the craziness that is going on at home.

When I come down for breakfast on Friday morning, Mom is gone.

"Are we really going back to Maine?" I ask Dad on the way to school.

"I don't know," he says. "Maybe . . . probably."

"What about school?"

"You and I won't be able to stay for more than a few days. You've got school and I've got work."

At school, I try to keep focused on my classes until lunch. Then, as I'm putting some books back in my locker, I see Kelly walking toward me through the crowd of students moving between their classes, lockers, and the lunchroom.

As she gets close, she half-smiles and says something. But it's so noisy, I can't make out if she's asking me a question or just saying hi, so I say, "What?"

"Come join us for lunch?" she says.

With all the noise and commotion swirling around me, I hesitate. She smiles one of her big Kelly smiles, and without warning she grabs my hand. When I realize what's happened, I pull it away. Then, still feeling confused, I follow her into the lunchroom.

It's actually noisier in the lunchroom than it is in the halls. Luckily, I brought my own lunch because today there's no way I want to tackle standing in a lunch line. I follow Kelly to a table way in the corner, where I see Mike and Nancy sitting.

"Are you going back to Maine?" asks Mike, as soon as I sit down.

"I don't know for sure yet. We're supposed to have a family meeting about it on Sunday." Then before I can say anything else Nancy asks, "Has there been news about your sister?"

I can see where this is going. I'm going to spend my lunch fielding questions from Mike and Nancy. This is all about my not going to the play.

"Not really," I say.

"Why are you going back if there hasn't been any news?" Mike continues.

"Mom really wants us to. I guess she thinks the authorities aren't doing enough to find Toby."

"What does your Dad think?"

"I think he's worried that going back won't accomplish anything."

Kelly has just been listening, but finally she asks, "Well, what do you think?"

"I don't know what to think. But I'm worried about missing school and choir rehearsals."

"I can understand that," says Nancy. "But if the authorities haven't been able to find Toby—that's her name right, Toby?—what can you guys do?"

"Actually, she thinks that we're the only ones who can find Toby."

"Yeah, sure," Mike says, looking confused.

"Mom says the authorities can't find Toby because they don't care enough."

"Wow," says Mike in disbelief. "Excuse me, but that sounds crazy."

I sigh before answering: "That's what she says."

I don't want to answer any more questions. I pick up my cheese and pickle sandwich and take a bite, but I'm not hungry.

"Well," says Kelly finally. "I guess I can kind of understand how she feels." She sounds sincere, but she doesn't know Mom, and she doesn't understand how crazy Mom's become.

Nobody says anything for a couple of minutes. We just sit there and eat as the lunch period slowly ticks away. Finally, Nancy brings up Kelly's play.

"It's too bad you can't come."

"Well, I can't," I say, as I take another bite of sandwich.

"Kelly is playing Jenny, the prostitute."

"Great," I say, "a starring role." Then, for some unknown reason, I add, "doesn't that role usually go to a soprano?" I had seen the play on public television a couple of years ago, and it seems to me that the actress who played Jenny was a soprano.

Kelly looks a little embarrassed. Then after a moment she says, "I was afraid I might have a little problem with the high parts. But my range is pretty wide, so Mr. Glenn worked with me, and I really think I'll do OK."

Can I visualize Kelly as Jenny? I'm not sure, but it's clear she is really excited about getting the role, and I don't want to rain on her parade.

"Too bad you can't come," Nancy says. "It's going to be great fun."

"Yeah, it sounds like it," I say. And it does sound like fun. "But it's out of the question now."

Now, I feel embarrassed that I can't go and that my family is in such a mess because of Toby's disappearance. If Toby had listened to me that day out on the little island, things would be so different. If she had just listened, and if I hadn't . . . I've got to leave. Luckily, the bell ending lunch sounds just as I get up to go. Then Kelly appears at my side and gives me a big hug.

"Good luck, Robin," she says. She smiles a little nervously and adds, "I mean, whatever happens, I hope you find Toby."

"Let me know if you're going, dude," Mike says, and then he gives me a high-five.

"I'll email you," I promise.

Nancy smiles and then she and Mike leave. Kelly stands there for a minute watching them disappear into the crowd of kids leaving the lunchroom.

"I wish you had a cell phone," she says finally.

"Yeah, me too," I reply. But I'm thinking, *maybe at this moment, it's better I don't.*

"I'll miss you at choir practice if you go back to Maine."

I feel a little uncomfortable. "I'll probably be back in a week or so," I say. "I can't afford to miss too many practices, or too much school."

On Sunday it's decided that we will fly back to Maine on Wednesday afternoon, October 8th, after Dad's class. Then Dad and I will fly back home on Monday, October 13th. I have to leave school early on Wednesday, and that means missing choir practice.

On Monday I get up early. I want to email Maude, to tell her that we are flying back. She still hasn't responded to my last email. But now that we'll be back in Maine, I really want to see her.

Dad talks to the school, explains the situation as best he can, and promises to get me back on the 14th. I'll get either Mike or Nancy to lend me their AP Environmental Science notes after I get back. October 13th is a holiday, so Dad doesn't have to get anybody to take his Monday class.

Mom doesn't get home until I'm up in my room getting ready for bed, and she's not up on Tuesday morning before I leave for school.

Both Dad and I try to sleep on the flight from Seattle on Wednesday afternoon. But Mom seems nervous, like she's got things she can't get off her mind. After I nod off, I wake up a couple of times and both times it looks she's talking to herself.

Bill picks us up at the airport at 1:00 a.m. It's surprisingly cold when we walk from the terminal to the parking garage to find Bill's car.

"A cold front just blew in from Canada," Bill says. "It's kind of early; usually our falls are pretty mild."

It's been a long day, and I don't get to bed until 3:00. So I sleep late, and when I finally come downstairs on Thursday morning, everybody else is sitting in Bill's kitchen. They've already eaten breakfast. Dad and Mom are drinking coffee, and Bill is doing the dishes. Everybody looks at me then I walk into the kitchen.

Mom frowns.

"Good morning, Robin," Bill says.

Then Dad adds, "I was just about to come upstairs to get you."

I get myself some cereal, berries, and milk. Almost immediately, Mom starts talking.

"Now that Robin's here, I want us to get organized for the next couple days. We're going over to Isle au Haut tomorrow morning, and we have to catch an early ferry, so we all need to get to bed early because tomorrow will be a long day."

"Today, your dad and I are going back up to Augusta at noon to talk with the state police, just see if they have any new information."

I wonder if this is Dad's idea. But the good news is I don't have to go. I'll stay here and help Bill prepare his garden for winter, which actually sounds a lot better than going to Augusta with Mom.

After Mom and Dad leave, Alice comes over, and the three of us work on covering plants and digging up some of the beds that will have to be replanted in the spring.

"It's a great thing your grandfather is doing, allowing us to use this property for an organic garden to help folks who don't have enough to eat," Alice says, after we've been working together for a while.

"Actually, it was Alice's idea originally," says Bill, "but I always used to remind my congregation that we will be judged more by our deeds than by our words. So giving the land, or at least the fruit of the land, over to help those in need seemed like an easy call. Anyway, it was your grandmother's garden. I haven't really kept it up the way I should. But with Alice and the other folks involved, it will be maintained properly, and will serve a larger purpose. So I think Helen would approve."

After about two hours we stop for lunch. While we are eating, Bill mentions that he wants the family to sing together on Sunday in honor of Toby.

"Oh," I say. I'm thinking, *This is a bad idea.*

"What do you suppose your parents will think of my idea?" Bill asks.

"I don't know about Dad, but Mom won't like it."

"Why?" Bill asks.

"It sounds like one of those parties the Irish have when somebody dies."

"A wake? Oh no, it wouldn't be a wake," Bill says." It's about doing something that we love—something that Toby loves too—and thinking about her when we do. It's about acknowledging your feelings, about forgiving ourselves, and preparing us all as a family for what might happen."

"Mom thinks we'll find Toby and that when we do everything will be back to normal."

"But Robin, what if we don't? And even if we do, what will we have learned?"

I don't know what to say. It's strange, but I hope that Mom's right because I'd give anything for things to be normal again. Maybe then it won't matter so much what happened on the island that day, but the idea of having a singing party when Toby is still missing just seems wrong. Still I know Bill is just doing his minister-thing, trying to help everybody feel better, so I don't respond to his questions. Instead, I change the subject.

"Is it OK if I call Maude?"

Bill frowns. "Do you have her number?" he asks.

"Yes, I do."

There's a pause, and then Bill says, "OK, but keep it short. And, you'll want use the landline in my study. It'll be more private that way."

Maude doesn't answer, so I leave a short message: "Hi Maude. This is Robin. Robin Steele. We're back at Bill's until Monday. When you get this message give me call. I'd like to hear from you."

I leave Bill's landline number and hang up.

Mom and Dad return from Augusta at about 4:00.

"Did the state police have anything new to say?" Bill asks, once everyone has gathered in the kitchen.

"Nothing. Nothing at all," Mom replies. She sounds really angry.

Then Dad adds, "They would rather we didn't spend a lot to time trying to search for Toby ourselves. But your mom is right—they had nothing new to share. Although they did give us a copy of the evidence report on Toby's hat."

Mom pulls out a piece of paper from the shoulder bag she always carries. "There's not much here, but it might help us a little bit when we get to the island."

I can tell that Mom is more determined than ever to go to Isle au Haut to search for any sign of Toby or any information about what happened to her. So tomorrow we're going. I just hope I can sleep some tonight.

CHAPTER TWENTY-SIX

Isle au Haut

Friday feels like an upside-down day right from the beginning. Visitors need to have reservations to go to the island, and we have to take the mail boat to get there. The boat, which runs to Isle au Haut just twice a day can only take about ten people at once. Bill made the reservations for Mom. He said we were lucky it was October. I guess interest in visiting the national park drops off after September.

The mail boat ferry leaves at 7:00 a.m., so we have to get up at 5:00. I really don't want to get out of bed that early, and I'm thinking, *Do we really have to do this?* We just barely make it to Stonington in time to catch the boat, which seems pretty small to me. Bill drops us off. He'll pick us back up at 5:00 p.m.

The trip takes about forty-five minutes. It's clear but cool, and even though I've brought a jacket, it's too cool to just sit. So I wander around the deck and spend some time listening to the captain. He's a talkative guy with grey hair and a beard, and he spends ten minutes telling the passengers about the history of the island.

It turns out that the boat, which was built to carry mail and other cargo to the island, provides the only year-round access to and from the island. There is a ferry that runs from May through September and on holidays. About sixty-five people live full-time on the island, mostly in the village called—you guessed it—Isle au Haut. The population doubles in the summer during the busy tourist season. The south half of the island is part of Acadia National Park, and the northern half is where the fishermen and people with summer homes live. According to the captain, tourists were flocking to the island by the 1970s. Then the locals demanded that the Park Service set up a reservation system to control the number of tourists on the island. And that's why only forty-eight day-trippers are allowed to visit the island each day.

The boat docks at Isle au Haut village landing. Dad wants to find a place where he can get a cup of coffee, but Mom is in a hurry and wants to check with the park ranger right away. So naturally we go to the information center first, which turns out to be a couple blocks from the landing. When we get there, it's closed, so we stand around and wait.

At a few minutes after 8:00, a middle-aged woman arrives and opens the information center. She's thin with little flecks of grey in her dark brown hair, which sticks out from under her ranger's hat. The name on her badge is Maria.

Mom takes the evidence report out of the little backpack Bill let us use. Then she asks Maria about some place called Robinson Point and, without waiting for her reply, hands her the report.

Looking a little confused, the ranger glances at the report.

"We're here because we think that the hat found on the beach at Robinson Point belongs to our daughter."

"I see," says the ranger. She pauses and then says, "Robinson Point is about two miles south. There's a dirt road that goes out there and a lighthouse and an inn at the point. But I can tell you something about what happened because the innkeeper brought the hat to me when it was found."

Mom looks surprised. "Do you know who found it and how we can get in touch with them?"

"It was a guest at the lighthouse. He found it on the beach and gave it to the innkeeper, who gave it to me."

Mom frowns. "Is it usual for the innkeeper to bring you things that are found on the beach?"

"Not really. It usually depends on where it was found—in the park or outside."

"This was found in Acadia National Park?"

"It was found a little below the Duck Harbor trail, on the beach fronting Moore's Harbor, just inside the park boundary."

"Did anyone go out there to see if there was anything else left on the beach?"

"When I saw the Amber Alert notice, I went out there myself. The rocky beach is easily accessible from the trail, and, of course, something like that hat could have been left on the beach or floated in from the harbor. Anyway, I didn't find anything else."

"Oh, the hat wasn't actually found at Robinson Point?"

"No, there is a frequently used beach called Goss Beach a little closer to Robinson Point, but that is outside the park boundary," says Ranger Maria.

"I'd like to know if the innkeeper can give us any more information and see where the guest found Toby's hat."

"The entrance to the Duck Harbor trail is right behind this building, and that's the trail that takes you right by the beach. It's about two miles to Robinson Point. You can rent bikes at the mail boat dock, or you can walk." Ranger Maria pauses. I can tell she's waiting to see what Mom thinks about spending the morning walking or biking to the inn.

Mom frowns. She is obviously impatient or unhappy with what she's being told.

"But if you want to wait until noon, I could take you with me when I go to the inn and then drop you off where the road meets the trail which is about a quarter of a mile from the place where the hat was found."

Mom sighs, and looks at Dad. "I'd really like to see where they found Tony's hat," she says.

Ranger Maria pulls out a trail map and shows Mom the approximate place where Toby's hat was found. "From the trail, it's an easy walk down to the beach. but be sure you're inside the park before you look for the beach. And the beach you want is quite rocky, so you'll need to be careful, especially if the tide is in."

Dad spoke up: "Is there any way to tell if the hat was dropped on the beach, or if it just washed in from the harbor?"

"Not really. But apparently, the guest who gave the hat to the innkeeper said that it was wet when he picked it up."

"I'd like talk to the innkeeper, and I really want to see where that guest found Toby's hat," Mom says again. "How long is the hike to the beach?"

"From the trailhead out back, it's a little over two miles."

"Claire, let's take the ranger up on her offer," Dad says. "We can get a cup of coffee and decide what we want to ask the innkeeper."

"We'll be wasting the whole morning," Mom replies.

"But we'll be better prepared."
To my surprise, Mom agrees.

The lighthouse stands on a rocky base and is attached to a small outcropping of land by a kind of walkway. On the landside of the walkway are some white wooden guest chairs, and right up against a big stand of spruce is a house, which is now an inn.

Ranger Maria drives us to the inn, and we get there a little after noon. The morning clouds and coolness have been replaced by bright fall sunshine, and the day feels warm enough that I pull off my jacket. Mom is completely wired, having drunk three cups of coffee at the little coffee cart by the town landing while she and Dad talked about what they could and couldn't accomplish by seeing where Toby's hat was found. I don't think they agreed.

The innkeeper is a woman named Casey, who must be in her twenties. Mom tells her our story. She seems to want to be helpful, but everything she says we've already heard from Ranger Maria. Yes, the hat was turned in by a guest, and the innkeeper says she doesn't keep guest information after they leave and have paid their bill. Mom questions this, but Casey just keeps telling us the same thing.

We leave the inn, and Ranger Maria drives us south to where the dirt road that zigzags around the island intersects with the Duck Harbor trail, about a mile and a half from the ranger station. There she drops us off.

This part of the trail winds southward through a beautiful forest of mixed spruce and deciduous trees. The leaves on many of the trees have turned red or reddish-yellow or bright yellow. Before long, we can see coastline and then a sandy strip of beach with a few of people on it. Dad says this must be Goss Beach, the public beach the Ranger Maria had told us about. We walk on and lose sight of the beach. Then in about ten minutes we pass a sign saying that we are now entering Acadia National Park.

Immediately, the beach comes back into view, but now it looks quite rocky. Ranger Maria told us to look for two large rocks, set about five feet apart just outside the tree line on the beach. We were to follow the visitor-made path running between them toward the beach. The guest who found Toby's hat had spotted it about halfway between the rocks and the water. He said it had been at low tide. But, of course, today the low tide will be at 5:00 p.m.

We end up walking around the area between the rocks and the shoreline, looking for anything that might have belonged to Toby, or that might give us a clue about what happened to her. The red, orange, and gold colors of the trees with the blue sky and blue-grey of the water make it a beautiful spot in the fall. There's almost no breeze, and the bay looks calm and peaceful. In other circumstances, I would say this place is perfect. But we've got other things on our minds, and after walking around on the rocks for a while, my legs ache, and I want to sit down. This isn't getting us anywhere. So I plop myself down on a flat rock. A couple of minutes later, first Dad and then Mom do the same thing. Dad talks softly to Mom and massages her shoulders, but I can tell she's not listening. She just stares out across the beach at the bay and rubs her forehead with her right hand.

I look around at the harbor and woods, thinking about the day I met Maude when we walked on the beach. I remember her telling me how much she loved Isle au Haut . . . Now I'm imagining myself hiking with her on the Duck Harbor trail, enjoying the scenic views, laughing, snuggling by a campfire, kissing and. . . . It would be so awesome to have her show me the island.

My daydreaming is interrupted when Dad says, "It's almost two. We should think about leaving."

Mom picks up a rock and stands up. "Shit!" she yells, and then tosses the rock as hard as she can into the water. It splashes and sends out ripples along the shore.

Neither Dad nor I know what to do or say.

"Hello," someone yells.

It's Ranger Maria. She's walking toward us from the trail.

"Did you find anything?" she asks when she gets close enough.

Mom stares at her. She looks totally wasted.

"Not really," says Dad.

"I went back and spoke with Casey again at the Inn."

"She didn't tell us anything really, nothing more than you already had," Mom says.

"But I think she was trying to be helpful," Dad adds.

"I'm sure she was," Maria says. "Anyway, the person who found the hat was an Indian man who was visiting friends in Portland. They paid for his lodging here, so Casey doesn't have any record of how to contact him."

Mom gives an audible sigh.

"But she's going to contact the person who charged the room, and if he's OK with you contacting him, she'll let you know. Or if he can give her more information, she will send it to you. You'll need to give me an email address or a telephone number where she can contact you. I'll give it to Casey when I see her on Monday."

Ranger Maria drives us back to the village in her park ranger pickup. She suggests we check out the little

Island Store, which is the only place where you can buy real food on the island. Mom jots down and hands Maria her email address and cell phone number.

"And if you hear anything new, anything, please let us know?" she adds.

"Sure," says Ranger Maria, "and I'll certainly notify the state police if anything else comes to my attention."

We get some salads, chips and some bottled water, and find a picnic table by the landing where we can eat. Nobody says much. Dad makes a comment that it might be nice to come back here sometime if we were visiting Bill. That makes me think of Maude. Mom doesn't say anything.

When we board the mail boat, the sun is almost on the horizon, and the wind has started to blow again, this time from the south. But the sky is still clear. I'm feeling really tired, and although there are no clouds in the sky, it feels like there is a big black cloud hanging over our family.

When we get back to Bill's, I'm not hungry. I just want to lie down. In my room, I rummage around in my backpack and pull out a copy of *Eagle Blue*, a book that Mr. Thom, the school librarian, recommended. It's about a bunch of native kids on a high school basketball team in a small Alaska town. I'm not much of a sports fan, but I like the way it tells the stories of the players and the coach and sets them against the backdrop of a struggling community. Those kids had a lot to overcome.

At some point I fall asleep—a restless sleep. In my dream, I see Toby running away from me, but I lose track of her in the bright sunlight. Then Mom yells at me from the steps of Bill's house: "Toby's gone." Or is she? Now I'm standing in a dark hallway. Someone shouts, "Look Robbie." It's Toby's voice. The only light is coming from underneath the door to her room. I stop at the door to listen. Nothing. I slowly open the door. The bright light of the room blinds me for just a second. When my eyes clear, I see that the room is empty, completely empty. Toby's photos, her posters, her clothes, everything that was Toby's is gone. I start to scream. Then I wake up shaking.

"I'd like us to take a break and get together Sunday afternoon to do some singing," Bill says at breakfast. "I think it would do us all some good."

Mom stares at her coffee, but I can see her frown. Dad puts down his copy of the Portland newspaper and looks interested.

"It would be nice to sing," Dad says. "We don't do that much anymore, and it always makes me feel happier."

Mom looks at Dad, but still doesn't say anything.

"So what do you think, Claire?" Bill asks.

"I know you're trying to be helpful, Bill. But right now, I've only got one thing on my mind, and that's finding Toby."

"Yes, well, I just thought that it might help to do something that we all love, something that could bring us together more as a family and give us a little more perspective on what's happening."

"I don't need a little more perspective. I know what's going on and what we need to do about it."

There's a pause and then Dad says, "I know you love to sing, Claire, and I know Toby loves to sing. So why don't we just try it and see if it might not help."

Mom's becoming agitated. "I'm beginning to think I'm the only one here who really wants to find Toby."

"That's not fair, Claire," Dad says. For a moment, it feels like Dad and Mom are going to get into an argument right here in the kitchen.

Then Bill speaks up: "Claire, we are all feeling anxious and fearful about Toby, and we're all asking questions none of us can really answer. But you're right: as a family we don't seem to be working well together. So singing together might help us prepare ourselves for what we're going to face, whether or not we find Toby."

Mom frowns at Bill. It's an angry frown. Dad looks at Mom and shakes his head. Bill looks sad, and I feel very uncomfortable. Why did Bill even bring this up?

"OK, Bill, have your sing along or whatever it is. Invite your girlfriend—what's her name—Alice. But I'm not going to participate."

Bill, Dad, and I sit stunned. How can we sing without Mom?

Bill sighs. "OK, Claire, but I hope you'll think about it. Music can be so healing, and it can bring us closer to each other. I, for one, will miss your wonderful alto voice in the mix."

"You're something Bill," Mom says. "I still remember when we came back to help you after Mom died. All you wanted to do was work in the garden and sing. It felt like you were trying to forget about Mom."

Bill's face turns white. Dad shifts around nervously in is chair.

"It made me feel closer to your mother," Bill says quietly.

"What?" Mom says. She looks dumbfounded.

"Working in the garden. It helped me feel closer to Helen." Bill pauses and then adds, "It was her garden, and whenever I worked in it, I felt like she was somehow there."

"And the singing? Mom never sang."

"I was singing *to* her. All those times when she sat with us in the circle, but didn't sing, I was singing to her. Hoping that she would join in."

"And now?" Mom asks coldly.

"I'm still singing to her—and now also to my granddaughter."

"OK," Mom says, "do whatever you want, but don't expect me to participate." She pauses and then adds, "And I want to say something else. It's clear to me that we are going to need to be here longer than just four days if we're going to find Toby."

"Claire, let's not go there now, please," Dad says.

But Mom is angry and she takes off full force.

"I don't understand you, Jim. Am I the only one who cares about finding Toby?"

"No, of course not, but look—" Dad says, only to be interrupted by Mom.

"We need to keep looking until we find her! And we need to stay here in Maine until we have found her—all three of us. Because we're the only ones who can do it!"

Dad stands up. "Be reasonable, Claire. We both have jobs, and Robin has to go back to school. If they'd found out something new, well—"

Mom interrupts again. "If we leave here now, we'll never find Toby. Is that what you want?"

"No," Dad says, "but we're not accomplishing anything here."

"We have a new lead, the person who found Toby's hat. We would never have gotten that information if we hadn't come back and if I hadn't insisted that we go out the Isle au Haut."

"Do you think that's really significant?"

"You're so negative about everything I try to do. I can't stand it any more. Go ahead if you want to. Go home. But I'm staying here until I find Toby, and Robin is staying with me."

What is she talking about? If I stay here, I won't be going to college next year, and I won't be singing at all.

"Claire, think about what you're saying. What about your job and Robin's school? He can't miss any more school if he expects to go to college next year."

"My job! Did you think about how important it was for you to keep your job when you were up for tenure?"

Dad gets a funny expression on his face. "You can't lose your job, Claire."

"It's too late. I already have."

"What?" Dad asks, his voice now strained from the stress of arguing with Mom. "What are you taking about?"

"I don't have a job. I wanted to take an indefinite leave of absence. I asked Dan and he said no. I worked Monday, and then at the end of the day, I quit."

Nobody says a word. Dad looks stunned. Bill sighs and rubs his forehead. My stomach hurts. Is this my mother talking, or someone who's gone completely nuts?

But Mom gets the last word. "That job has already cost me so much. I wasn't going to let it keep me from finding my daughter."

CHAPTER TWENTY-SEVEN

Gone

I wake up on Saturday thinking that everything—Toby's disappearance and everything surrounding it—has just been a dream. We are back in Seattle and Toby is about to come into my room to wake me up. I even smile knowing she'll be her same old annoying self. But then it hits me—I'm still in Maine and nothing has changed. Everyone is upset and angry with everyone else. Mom is acting crazy, and she's mad at both Dad and me. Dad is mad at Mom and a little at me I think, and Bill is upset at all of us for "not listening to each other." And even worse, I realize that I don't have the slightest idea what's going to happen next.

Right away I hear voices and I think Dad and Mom are arguing. But it turns out to be Bill and Alice working out in the garden. "Storm's coming this afternoon," I hear Alice say in her distinctive New England accent. "But it's likely too early for a big nor'easter, so it should clear out by tomorrow."

I look out the bedroom window. Alice and Bill are just below me in the backyard. Bill is smiling. Alice walks over to him and they hug. She says something else, but I can't hear what it is. Then she turns to head back to her car.

"See you tonight," Bill says as she is leaving.

I finally come downstairs about ten o'clock. Mom is sitting at the computer with the Amber Alert site filling the screen. It looks like everybody else has eaten. I don't see Dad or Bill. I'm finishing up my cereal when Bill comes back into the kitchen to get a cup of coffee. He says hi, but before I can ask him if he thinks we're going to stay in Maine, Dad comes out of Bill's study.

"What's going to happen?" I ask as he comes into the kitchen.

He sits down across from me. I must look pretty tired because he asks me if I'm OK.

"A little tired."

"Yeah," Dad says. Then he shakes his head, as if to say, *what a mess*! "I'm not sure if anyone slept very well last night, but I want you to know that you and I, at least, are going back to Seattle on Monday. I just got through making our reservations. So don't worry—you won't be missing any more school. And I don't want you to worry about everything else that is going on either."

"What about Mom?"

"I'm not sure, but whether she comes or not, you and I are flying back. You have to get back for school, and I have to get back to work."

"Mom quit her job," I say. "That's crazy!"

Dad sighs. "Well, she's very upset. This thing has become an obsession to her, and she's really the only person who can explain why she feels the way she does. That's why I think—why I really wish—you and she had talked about your feelings about what happened on that island. Anyway, now it's become a family affair."

"You think this is all my fault, just like Mom."

Dad doesn't respond directly. "Right now, all we can do is try to support your mom and help her through her grief, but we also can't shirk our responsibilities."

There's an awkward pause. I want to say something about how frustrating this whole mess has been, about how I'm being punished for something that wasn't my fault.

"Wake up, Robbie." The words seem way off now, and yet I understand that they are really inside my head. Why do I keep hearing them? I stop myself before I say anything, and Dad leaves the kitchen and heads back into the study.

"All three of you need to talk about what happened," Bill says after Dad leaves. "You haven't done that and it's been a mistake."

How many times has Bill said this same thing? Maybe he's right, but Dad's right too: it's a family affair. It's always been a family affair. I'm feeling trapped, almost like I'm paralyzed. I don't know what to say or do. I get up and pour myself half a cup of coffee. Maybe that will help me to wake up. Then, after a minute, I remember Maude. Why hasn't she tried to contact me?

"Did Maude come by or call yesterday?" I ask.

"No," Bill says, and he frowns.

"You're not trying to contact that girl are you?" It's Mom. She's standing in the doorway looking very tired and angry. "You should be ashamed of yourself, absolutely ashamed. We're here to find Toby, and all you can do is mope around and try to contact some girl you met once here on the beach. Well, you're forbidden to see her. Do you understand?"

She's almost yelling, and that's scaring me. I could tell her that Maude and I have exchanged emails, but that would probably make things worse.

"I just don't understand you, Robin. You don't seem to care about anybody but yourself."

I feel funny again, like I'm going to be sick.

"Claire." It's Dad. He's come out of Bill's study. "Claire, can we talk?"

Mom stands there glaring at me. And I get the message—this is all my fault. Finally, she turns and heads past Dad and into the study. Almost immediately, I hear loud voices coming from behind the study door. Bill and I stand in the kitchen listening. Then, after a couple minutes, Mom storms out of the study. She grabs her coat and heads out the door.

We walk to the front window and watch her walk down to the beach. Dad joins us at the window. Mom is standing at the shoreline staring out at the little island. Clouds have been rolling in all morning, and the wind is picking up. Shadows have started moving across the water and the island. As we watch, Mom seems to be looking at something on the island—maybe a bird or maybe just a shadow. Suddenly she turns and walks quickly toward Bill's canoe.

"No, Claire!" Dad says. He heads out the front door.

I'm a little confused. What's going on?

"Go with him, Robin," says Bill.

I want to ask him what's going on, but he stops me.

"Go, Robin. Just go."

By the time I get to the front steps, Dad has almost caught up to Mom, who is trying to push the canoe into the water. Now I understand what's happening—Mom wants to go out to the island.

As I head toward the beach, I hear Dad yell, "No, Claire!"

"I've got to find Toby," Mom exclaims loudly, and she points out at the island. "She's out there somewhere."

She's in the canoe now and as he reaches her, Dad grabs her arm. She tries to push him away, but his grip is too tight.

"She's not out there, Claire. She's gone."

"She has to be," Mom says again. "I don't know where else to look. Where else can I look, Jim?"

For a moment, everything seems to stop. Mom and Dad seem to be frozen. I seem to be frozen too. Even the wind stops, only to pick up again as it starts to rain. As I get to them, Mom goes limp in Dad's arms.

Am I responsible for all this? If only Toby had listened to me and stayed away from the water. If only I hadn't gone to sleep. If only . . .

We walk slowly back toward the house, me slightly behind my parents. As we near the steps, the rain gets heavier. At the front door Mom turns to me—she looks so sad—and she says, "Where can we look for her, Robin? Where can we look?"

"I don't know Mom" is all I can say.

A Lullaby for Toby

The storm hits. It's raining heavily when I go up to my bedroom. I pick up the book I'd stuck into my backpack as we left the house on Wednesday morning. It's *The Absolutely True Diary of a Part-Time Indian*. I'm having a hard time getting into it. I don't read much fiction, and I can't stop thinking about seeing Mom fall apart. After a few minutes, I put down the book and start thinking about Maude and then about food.

I go downstairs and find Dad and Bill talking quietly in the kitchen. I make the mistake of asking Bill if I can use his telephone to call Maude's cell phone. Dad immediately vetoes the idea.

"You need to stay with the family while we're here," he says. "You're a big part of what's happened, and right now we need you to stay focused on helping out the family, particularly your Mom."

That's the closest Dad has come to saying that I'm responsible for Toby's disappearance. Sure, I am concerned about Mom, but I can't really do anything to help, can I? And I've got this girl on my mind. I'd like to see her and find out why she hasn't tried to contact me.

"I was just thinking maybe I could invite her to the sing-along. She plays the violin, and I bet she's good."

Dad glares at me and says, "This get-together is for family, Robin, not for strangers."

"Well, Alice is coming." The minute I say that I know it is a mistake.

Dad glances over at Bill and then back at me. "Don't argue with me on this, Robin," he says. "We hardly even know this girl. And it would just upset your mother."

I look at Bill, hoping he will say something positive about Maude, or just say that it's OK with him if she comes. But he doesn't say anything. *This sucks.* That's what I want to say, but I don't.

I get an apple and some milk from the kitchen. Then I go back to my bedroom and try to read some more. But I just can't seem to concentrate. Then I remember something. Maude was going to be in Providence one weekend in early October, interviewing for an internship. Shit! If it's this weekend, maybe she doesn't even know I'm here. Still, if I was able to call her cell phone, I could leave a message, and maybe we could still connect on Sunday night. I've got to try.

By four o'clock, Bill's house is quiet, except for the noise of the wind and the rain outside. With apparently nobody around, I decide to take my shot. As I pass Mom and Dad's bedroom, I hear them talking—so maybe the coast is clear. Then I go downstairs and find Bill talking quietly on the telephone. I go into the kitchen so it won't look like I'm just hanging around. When I hear him put down the receiver, I come out.

"Bill, can I use the telephone?"

"Is this to call Maude?" he asks.

I nod.

"You know what your Dad said."

"I don't think it's fair. All I want to do is talk with her."

"Well, I can't let you use the telephone to call Maude. You'll have to get your parents' OK for me to do that.

But I was just talking with Maude's father—that's who I was on the telephone with—and he said Maude is in Providence interviewing for an internship. He's not sure when she'll be back, but he said he'll let her know you're here when he sees her."

Wow! Bill called Maude's father for me. For a moment, I don't know what to say. So I blurt out, "Did he say anything else?"

"I didn't question him. He asked about Toby, and I didn't want to get into a big discussion with him about our family. As for you, Robin, I wouldn't push this idea about seeing Maude any more today. Wait and hope that Maude contacts you."

I feel relieved though still unhappy. Bill saved me by calling Maude's father, and now I know she's in Providence. But if I could have called her and left a message, she'd know I want to see her. This way, I'm less sure I'll see her before we leave.

I go back upstairs to lie down and read some more, but I can't focus. I start thinking about what I want to say to Maude if I actually get to see her. I shift onto my side, and it's then I see the photograph on the little bookshelf that sits in the corner on the wall side of the bed. It's of Toby and me walking together across a wooden bridge over a stream of roaring water.

Immediately I remember where we were. The photograph is from last summer. We had gone to Mount Rainier on a camping trip. But how did it get here? Did Mom send it to Bill? I vaguely remember her saying that she was sending a few pictures of the two of us to Bill last fall. She said he wanted some newer pictures of his grandchildren.

Toby loved to camp although she'd always complain when she couldn't have her favorite food while we were living in a tent. Anyway, she was really excited about seeing Mount Rainier up close, and on the first full day we were there, she bugged us all morning about taking a hike. It was typical Toby. So around noon, Mom and I decided to take her on what we thought would be a short hike along a trail that ran parallel to the small river just outside the campground. We were going to walk to a point where we could see a small waterfall and let Toby take some pictures. About halfway to the falls, the trail crossed the river. But the bridge over the river had been washed out in a flood, and to replace it, the rangers cut down a big tree, made it flat on one side, and dropped it over the water. They'd put a railing on the right side of the tree bridge and nothing on the left.

Mom took the lead as we started across the bridge. For safekeeping, she had Toby's camera. Toby was in the middle and I was at the back. I took a few steps onto the bridge and looked down. The bridge looked slick and the rushing water seemed so far below us. I looked up and saw that Mom had already made it to the end. I took a few more steps. I knew I shouldn't look down again, but I couldn't help myself. My heart started to pound. I looked down and froze.

"Go back if you have to," I heard Mom yell. But I couldn't move.

"Take my hand, Robbie." It was Toby. I remember thinking, *Why isn't she scared*?

"Take my hand," she said again and immediately grabbed my hand. Panicked, I started to pull away from her, but I couldn't move.

"Don't look down Robbie—follow me." Then she turned and took one step forward, then another.

"Don't look down," she said again. "Take a deep breath and follow me."

So, haltingly, I followed my little sister one step at a time across the bridge.

"Good job, Robin," Mom said when I got to the other side.

So the picture is not of Toby and me walking across the bridge together. It is of Toby guiding me across after I froze up in the middle of the bridge.

The other thing I remember about that day is that when I stumbled off the bridge, and after Mom had asked me how I was, I noticed Toby standing beside Mom with her hands on her hips

"Were you scared?" she asked.

"A little," I said, trying to down play what had just happened.

"Well," Toby said, "from now on don't be such a scaredy-cat."

It was classic Toby. Only this time I wasn't cross at her at all. I looked at the picture of Toby leading me across the bridge and smiled. She was just a little girl, but she was fearless enough to help her big brother when he really needed it.

Thinking back to last summer, all I wanted was for Toby to be here, so that I could tell her how brave she was and give her a big hug. But she wasn't here and she might never be again.

Oh Toby. I'm sorry.

It's Sunday morning. The rain has stopped, and the sun is peeking through the clouds. But when I walk outside, there's a winter chill in the air, even though it's early October. The wind last night knocked most of the leaves off the trees surrounding the house.

Alice comes over after lunch and brings her violin. So there are four of us—Alice, Bill, Dad, and me—who finally sit down in the living room to sing. Bill has an extra guitar that he gives Dad to use. Then the three of us—Alice, Dad, and I—all look at Bill. It's his party, so he has to get it started.

"Today," he says, "I want us to sing songs that we love, and I want us to think about Toby as we're singing and to sing some of the songs that she loves. So let's start with one of those, "Mrs. Murphy's Chowder.""

It stays kind of like that for a while. Each person suggests a song that they like or is special to them, and we sing it. We do "Forever Young," "Rocky Mountain High," "Riding on the City of New Orleans," "The Erie Canal Song" (a Toby favorite), "If I had a Hammer," "Singing for our Lives," and "Goodnight, Irene."

Just as we start singing "Goodnight, Irene," I hear a new voice joining in. Bill and Dad look in my direction and Bill is smiling. My heart jumps as I recognize that strong alto sound. It's Mom and she's standing right behind me.

When we finish, Bill asks Mom to suggest a song. There's a long pause before she says, "Morning Morgantown." It's a lively bouncing song and gets us moving along and on to some more traditional stuff, "Railroading on the Great Divide" and "This Land is Your Land." Then Dad suggests another Toby favorite, "James James Morrison Morrison," based on the poem by A.A. Milne. She knows the words by heart, and I remember hearing her sing it sometimes in her room, or in the kitchen when no one else was around. It is a fun song, but as we're singing it, I realize Mom has stopped singing.

Then it's my turn. I feel like I want to dedicate something to Toby. "This song is for Toby," I say. "It's called 'The Brandy Tree.'" At that moment, I notice that everybody is looking at me, and it seems like they're expecting me to say more about Toby or about the song. I start and stop and stumble over my words, and finally get something out.

"Toby was . . . is a playful kid who enjoys life just like the otter in this song."

To save myself from more embarrassment, I immediately start to sing. Bill and Dad, and then Alice, and finally Mom join in, and for the first time, I feel like we're all singing together—different voices, different parts, but all folding together and sounding just right. I can even hear a harmony.

When it's Mom's turn again, she passes, which feels like a let-down. Alice passes too, which brings us to Dad.

"I want to sing something for Toby, too," he says. "It's a song by Gordon Bok, who also wrote 'The Brandy Tree.' It's appropriate since it's about a place in Maine. It's called the 'Isle au Haut Lullaby.'"

Right away, I can tell that Bill knows the song, too. He and Dad are leading us. And I remember us singing it a couple times at home, so I'm able to follow along, while Alice plays a nice violin accompaniment. By the second stanza in the chorus, we've got everything sounding right, except that, again, there's one voice missing. Just as we get to the last lines in that part of the chorus, "Give sadness to the stars, Sorrow to the sea,"[2] I hear what sounds like a moan. The singing stops, and I turn around. Immediately, Mom slumps into me. I put my arms around her, and she does the same to me. At first, I think she's steadying herself, but then she won't let go. She's hugging me and she's crying.

"Oh, Robin, you're not the only one who let her down. I let her down too." For the first time since Toby disappeared, she looks me straight in the eyes. Hers are red and her face is full of pain. She continues to cry.

What's she talking about?

"We both let Toby down and now she's lost."

I feel dizzy. "What?" I say. Then I feel someone else's hand on my back. It's Dad. His face too is pinched with pain.

"Claire," Dad says. "Do you want to take some time to compose yourself?"

"No, I've got to say this now. I've got to say it, or I'm afraid I'll die, and especially I've got to tell Robin."

Now Bill and Alice are standing next to Dad. And we are all looking at Mom.

"I was too preoccupied with my work. I had this damn big sale I was trying to complete, and there were last-minute problems, so when I called Dan that morning, what was supposed to be a five-minute call just went on and on, and I just forgot . . . I forgot what I was supposed to do."

Mom stops as if she's catching her breath, or deciding what else she wants to say.

"Can I have a drink of water?" she asks.

After a minute, someone—I'm not sure who—hands her a glass. She drinks it as if she's dying of thirst. She's stops crying and seems to be more herself.

"Your dad and I talked that morning, and I was supposed to talk with you before you and Toby left."

"Talk?"

"About the tides. Your dad asked me to talk with you because he and Bill wanted to leave, and he didn't want to just leave the tide table on the kitchen table for fear that you wouldn't look at it."

"But what about the note?"

"There was no note," Dad says. He's put his arm around Mom and is simultaneously trying to comfort her and talk to me.

"No note? But there was a piece of paper with my name on it. I saw it."

"I started to write you a note, but then I was afraid you either wouldn't see it or wouldn't read it, so I asked your mom to tell you there was going to be a very high tide around one o'clock that afternoon. I knew Toby would be pestering you to go."

Mom has gotten herself a little more under control. "And I was supposed to talk with you and then make a decision about whether or not it was OK for you two to go. But I was talking on the phone to Dan and lost track of time. When I went to find you, you and Toby were gone. And once you were gone, I didn't know what else to do. I couldn't get out to the island, but I could have . . . should have tried. So you see, it's really my fault Toby is missing, my fault as much as yours."

I hear what Mom is saying, but I don't believe it. And then, as I think about it, I start to believe it—or at least I can understand—how it could have happened. Does that mean that Mom is responsible for what happened? Not really.

"It's not your fault, Mom," I say. "I fell asleep."

Suddenly, I feel like something very heavy has been lifted off my chest. I feel relieved but also very sad. "Mom, I should have taken better care of Toby. It was my responsibility and I let her down. And now, I don't know what to do to make it right. How can we make it right?"

"I think that's what all of us are struggling with right now," says Dad. I see tears in his eyes.

"The truth is, I'm just as much responsible for what happened as you or your mom. I shouldn't have left it to her to tell you about the high tide. I should have come upstairs, woke you up, and told you myself. I shouldn't have left you a note or asked your mom to do it. I should have done it myself."

Now I am crying, and Mom pulls me tight against her. It reminds me of the hugs she used to give me as a child when I was hurt or scared. And for some reason, I suddenly feel like everything is going to be OK, even though I know it never can completely be, not even if we find Toby alive.

Chapter Twenty-Nine

The Osprey

The big bird tucks its wings along its sides and watches the two-legged creatures on the island. The bigger one is sitting by the small tree at the center of the island. The smaller one is walking along the shore. The big one makes some noise. The smaller one looks back toward the bigger one and then turns around and starts walking back toward the sunrise side of the island.

The bird likes to hunt along this part of the shore. The swift current along the channel just off the little island is a good place to search for fish. But he has been hunting all morning without much success and now rests in the big tree, watching the two-legged creatures on the island. The small creature is now in the water just off the east shore. The large creature is lying quietly by the tree. As the water rises, the small creature is having trouble keeping its balance.

Then the bird notices a flash of light in the bay not far from the island. He opens his wings and pushes himself off from the tree with his strong legs. He wants to get a closer look. If he is quick enough maybe he can catch a lunch.

He sweeps down toward the water. His focus is on finding fish, but he sees no fish. Then he notices an odd wave. It moves below him and along the far side of the island. The bird turns around, and he sees the small two-legged creature just below him.

"Look, Robbie!"

Whoosh. Splash.

The bird turns away to sail off over the bay. Water splashes behind him. He makes a broad turn and looks again for fish. He finds nothing and then notices just to the south one of the funny-shaped objects he often sees moving over the water. The bird circles over the island. The small two-legged creature is gone. Below, the larger creature is still lying quietly by the tree.

CHAPTER THIRTY

Wake Up Robin!

It's hard to sleep after the drama of the afternoon. I toss and turn, fall in and out of odd dreams, and then I wake up. It's still dark. All the crazy things that have happened since we came back to Maine are tumbling through my mind.

"Robbie." Somebody's calling my name.

I crawl out of bed. For a moment, it seems like the room is upside down. Maybe I'm still dreaming. No one else is there. But then I hear the voice again.

"Robbie, wake up."

The voice sounds familiar. I look out of the bedroom window. Heavy dew is on the ground, and a small shaft of early morning sunlight is creeping into the garden. As it flickers and becomes brighter, I can barely make out a figure standing beyond the garden just in front of the trees. I think it's a girl. She looks so small. My heart jumps. It feels like it is going to explode.

"Toby," I blurt out. "Toby, I'm coming." But I'm shaking so hard I can't move. Then I hear the voice again.

"Robbie, come look."

Maybe there's still time to save her. Maybe if I can reach her, I can hold onto her and she'll be OK. I have to try. I fall down trying to pull on my jeans. I pull myself up and run down the stairs. I trip at the bottom. Up again, I run through the kitchen and out the back door. The coldness of the morning air catches me by surprise. The ground feels wet under my bare feet.

Sunlight has now spread across the half of the garden not shaded by the house. After a few more steps, I realize that the figure isn't Toby.

"Robin, come look at the sunrise." It's Maude. She looks just the way she did the first time I saw her sitting and sketching by the bay, slender and beautiful, with the sun highlighting her black hair.

"It's almost over, come on."

My heart stops pounding. I'm not having a nightmare, and Toby hasn't returned to let me save her. It's Maude, spectacular as ever, come to see me before I fly home. I sigh, then smile, and walk toward her.

"Are you OK?" she asks. "You look awful."

"No, you just roused me out of a bad dream." I move closer to her. Her violet eyes are sparkling in the morning sun.

"I had to go down to Providence to have my internship interview on Friday, and afterwards the person I interviewed with asked me to stay over and work with her in her studio on Saturday. I didn't get back home until late last night. But I wanted to make sure I got to see you before you left."

"How did it go?"

"Fine, I think," Maude says. Then she hugs me. "It's good to see you. I'm sorry I couldn't get back sooner, but I really want this internship. And I couldn't pass up a chance to work with this woman. She's doing fantastic stuff."

"I understand." I'm happy she came. I really wanted to see her, even if it is for only a few minutes on the last day I'll be here. "Things are kind of a mess here," I say.

"Oh, I'm sorry," she says, and she touches my hand. That's all the encouragement I need to start telling her everything that's happened over the few days.

But before I really get started, she smiles and says, "Let's take a walk on the beach."

I realize when she says it that I have to tell someone where I'm going or my parents will go crazy. "Can you walk inside with me for a minute?"

"Sure," she says.

Dad is sitting alone at the kitchen table drinking coffee. He looks up when we walk in. I can tell he's a little surprised to see Maude.

"Hi, Mr. Steele," Maude says.

"We're going for a walk on the beach," I say.

"Up kind of early, aren't you?" he says. I'm not sure if he's asking Maude or me. But it's Maude who answers.

"I'm an early riser, and I wanted to see Robin before he left."

Dad frowns. "Well, make it short. I'm making breakfast for the family."

"Sure," I reply. Of course, once we get on the beach, it won't be easy to keep track of time. I run upstairs and put on a long-sleeved shirt and some shoes. When I get back to the kitchen, Maude is telling my dad about her interview.

Then, out of the blue, as we are about to leave, Dad asks, "Do you want to join us for breakfast, Maude?"

"Well . . ." She hesitates and glances at me. Can she tell by the look on my face that I want her to stay? Maybe, because after a moment she says, "Sure."

"Come back in an hour, then," Dad says. "I'll work on slow-cooking breakfast."

The bay sparkles in the morning sun, and the sky is crystal clear. But the wind is cold, and I'm glad I brought a jacket. As we walk, I tell Maude everything that has happened since August. She listens intently.

"Still no good news about your sister?" Maude asks when I'm through.

"No, I suspect the sheriff thinks Toby was pulled out into the bay by some kind of freak wave. But Mom's not buying it. That's why we came back—to try to find something that would give us, particularly Mom, hope."

"And how about you? How are you doing?"

"I just have so many questions about what happened out on the island that day. Why didn't I stay awake and watch Toby better? Why didn't she listen to me when I told her to stay away from the water? Why was Mom so wrapped up in her work that she forgot to talk to me before we left for the island? Why didn't Dad realize that if he wanted to tell me something, he needed to tell me himself? And most importantly, what actually happened to Toby? Questions, but not answers."

We stop and stare out at the bay, using our hands to shield ourselves from the bright glare of the sun. The cold breeze has died down. I turn toward her, and she smiles softly at me. We're so close I could easily touch her, but I don't.

Then Maud says, "I've got this favorite poem that I read whenever I'm struggling with big life questions. It's called 'Letters to a Young Poet.' In it, Rilke says that while young artists are full of questions, they can't know the answers to any of them. He says that only through experience will we find the answers. So, we must learn to 'live the questions.'"[3]

She pauses and squeezes my hand. "For the longest time, I wanted more than anything to know why my mother left us. In my mind, I felt it was somehow because of me. Maybe I'd been bad. She must have been disappointed in me somehow. I didn't get any answers until a couple of years ago when Dad told me Mom was living in New York City. He let me take the train down to see her. And you know what— nothing I'd assumed to be true actually was true. In the end, all she could tell me was 'that she left to find herself.'

"Anyway, Robin, you can't escape your questions. But you can't stop living either. Because I think Rilke is right—it's only when we live our questions that we find the answers."

Breakfast goes OK. Maude talks about art school, and her dream of moving away from Belfast. Bill talks about his dream of building a sustainable garden to help feed the poor and says that if I want to come back after school's out, he can put me to work harvesting vegetables. I talk about how I'm both excited and nervous about soloing and about my dream of becoming a paleontologist. Dad mostly listens. Mom doesn't say anything, except, "It's important to have dreams."

After breakfast, I walk Maude back to the beach.

"When will you hear about your early action applications?" she asks.

"I guess in January. Of course, I still might apply to Berkeley or even Yale."

Maude gives me a raised eyebrow look when I mention applying to Yale.

"Yeah, it probably won't happen. Think you'll be around if I come back at the end of June?"

Maude shrugs. "I kind of doubt it. I want to get an apartment in Providence for the summer, if I can."

Suddenly I feel totally deflated. Will I ever see Maude again?

"But if you let me know when you're coming and how long you'll be here, maybe I can come up to see you, or maybe we can meet in Providence." She pauses and then adds, "I really need to get away from this place and be out on my own."

"Yeah, I know, but I want to keep in touch," I say.

"Sure," she says, but the way she says it makes me think that she's wondering if that can really happen. "Maybe you'll finally be able to get a cell phone once your parents know you're really going to college."

We both smile at the thought of me finally getting a phone.

"I'll email you to let you know where I get accepted."

We're almost to her house, and I can see the little concrete steps that lead from her property to the beach, where I first saw her sitting that Friday in August when I was trying to run away from what had happened.

"I want to sit and draw for a while," Maude says.

I know she's telling me that she wants to be alone, but I don't want to go. We stand there for a minute or two, and then she gives me a final hug.

"Anyway, don't beat yourself up too much, Robin Steele. You're a good person who made a mistake, and I know you feel shitty about it. But we all make mistakes, and life goes on."

"Yeah, I know what Toby would say if she was here to pester me."

Maude gets an odd expression on her face. "What would she say?" she asks.

"She'd say 'Wake up Robin, wake up.'"

We look at each other. Maude shrugs and then smiles. It's a sort of a sad smile. And suddenly I badly want to see or talk with her again before I leave.

"I'll call you tonight if I get a chance," I say.

"Sure," she says, "I'll be around."

Dad and I fly home tomorrow. Mom will stay for another week. I try calling Maude again after we finish packing, but it's late and she doesn't answer her cell.

CHAPTER THIRTY-ONE
January

I know what you're hoping to hear. That we found Toby alive and well. But that hasn't happened, at least not so far.

I went back to school and to choir after we got home, and Dad went back to his twenty-four-hour per week teaching job at the community college. Then Mom returned home without Toby. In November, Barack Obama was elected the forty-second president of the United States. If that had happened three months earlier, there would have been so much cheering and celebration at our house. Even though we all watched the election night coverage, we were pretty quiet as the returns came in. And when the networks declared that Obama the winner, Dad just said, "Maybe things will be better now." I guess that was something we could all sort of agree on.

The holidays were rough. We went out to eat on Thanksgiving. The choir held their holiday concert the first Wednesday of December. It turned out to be the only really happy part of the season. Both Mom and Dad came. Then two days before Christmas, Dad and I went out and got a small tree. In past years, Toby and I had decorated the tree after Dad put on the lights. But this year it was just Dad and I, and our hearts weren't really in it. Aunt Donna came over to help us make dinner. When Dad started to say a prayer for Toby at dinner, Mom left the table. Besides that, it was a quiet dinner.

I got a funny Christmas card from Maude, and I sent her a long email right after Christmas. She's totally into her plan to leave Belfast and attend college. Dad says they are going to get me a cell phone, as soon as they can budget for the purchase. And if that happens, I know the first person I'm going to call.

After the holidays, I started seeing Mr. Moore again. We've had some good discussions.

I got accepted at Western and the University for next fall. I haven't decided where I'll go. I did so well in both my fall AP classes, I'm still thinking about applying to Berkeley. But whatever happens, I can understand now how Maude felt about leaving home. I'm ready to move out when I start classes.

When I sent Maude a short email after I got my acceptances, she responded with a smiley face emoji email that just said, "Congrats."

Dad was offered a temporary job teaching at Western, starting in April. Since Mom still hasn't gone back to work, he had to accept it. He'll be staying in Bellingham four days a week and coming home on weekends, maybe through the summer. As for Mom, she has never really stopped looking for Toby. She is seeing a therapist, too, and she's mostly stopped blaming me for what happened to Toby. I think she just blames herself now.

She does the housework, cooks, and keeps on me about working hard at school. But she never laughs, and sometimes at night, if I get up to use the bathroom, I'll notice the light is on in Toby's room, and I know Mom is in the room.

I'm working hard with Mrs. Walker to prepare my solo for March. I don't have a curfew on weekends, so I'm hanging out with Mike, Nancy, and Kelly a lot. Kelly and I have had coffee a couple times, and she's invited me to the West High Players' next play, *The 25th Annual Putnam County Spelling Bee*. It's a musical comedy, and she's playing a middle school contestant with an attitude. I've thought about inviting her to go to a movie. But I don't want this to become a girlfriend/boyfriend thing—not yet anyway.

When I think of Maine, I think of Bill, and Maude, and Toby—two people that I hope will be in my life in the future, and one that I may never see again but will never forget.

I'm sorry, Toby. I don't know what else to say, though 'sorry' doesn't seem like enough. I guess for now I'll just have to live my questions. But maybe someday, if you come back, I'll be able to do more.